Falling for a Santini is never easy…

She made a sound that was halfway between a growl and a shout.

"Good lord, just go, JT. You made your position clear. I'm a big girl. You would have kissed any woman back who had locked lips with you. Now, could you leave so I can go disinfect my mouth, because you are apparently a whore with your mouth?"

He hesitated, then turned to walk to the door. He stepped up to the threshold, but…he couldn't do anything. No matter what he told himself, he couldn't force himself to take that last step away from her.

Even though he knew he shouldn't do it, he turned and looked at her one last time. She wasn't crying, wasn't smiling. Just nothing. And that told him one thing.

She was lying.

Instead of walking out the door, he slammed it shut and turned to stride in her direction. Her eyes widened as she dropped her hands down to her sides. He slipped his arm around her waist and yanked her against him. She gasped.

"This time, I'll do the kissing," he said.

Before he could have second thoughts, he crushed his mouth down on hers and damned them both.

Praise for the Santini Series!

Leonardo:
I can't wait to read about the next Santini brother
.-Ms Romantic Reads

Marco:
I love these brothers, and each and every one of them intrigues me.-For the Love of Bookends

Gianni:
This is a quick smoking hot read from one of my favorite authors. Ms. Schroeder has intimate knowledge of the military and brings that realism to her stories. -In My Humble Opinion

Vicente:
I very much enjoy Vincente and felt it was a good ending to this series.

-Guilty Pleasures Reviews

A Santini in Love: I loved seeing these two find each other again and fall hard.

-Smutty Kitty Reviews

Praise for Melissa Schroeder's Harmless Series

A Little Harmless Fascination is one of my favorite of the Harmless series. It has some incredibly hot moments as well as some wonderfully tender ones. It is a great romantic read.
Jennfier, RNN

A LITTLE HARMLESS SUBMISSION was just about perfect to me. It had the perfect mix of sexual tension, eroticism, suspense and cheekiness that I've come to associate with Melissa Schroeder's writing.
Rho, TRR

INFATUATION is an awesome contemporary, erotic and military romance that was such a joy to read, I finished it in 24 hrs while having to work. It was sizzling hot and emotional.
Pearl's World of Romance

Praise for Melissa Schroeder's Cursed Clan series

First thought when finished: Holy Cow! This is going to be a fun series to read---just the right combo of story/romance!
Felicia, The Geeky Blogger's Book Blog

This is a great Paranormal Romance novel! The dynamics of the McLennan clan are remarkable, the characters are impassioned and compelling, the plot is riveting and the delivery is faultless.
Smitten with Bad Boys Heroes

Falling For a Santini

Melissa Schroeder

ISBN:**1508817715**

ISBN-13:**978-1508817710**

DEDICATION

To my niece Kristen and her new husband Cory. May your life together be filled with love and laughter and all things that are beautiful and bright.
~Your crazy Aunt Mel

MILITARY TERMS

Annapolis: Naval Academy-College for the Navy and Marines

BOOT: Bootcamp

BX-Base Exchange: Air Force idea of a department store

Commissary: Military Grocery Store on base

Deployment: When someone is sent to work usually in hostile areas, but they still have a permanent base at home they are assigned to.

IED: Improvised Explosive Device

Joint Base/Assignment: Base or assignment that has more than one service involved

MCAGCC: Marine Corps Air Ground Combat Center

MCEX: Marine Corps Exchange

NEX-Naval Exchange: Navy idea of a department store

OCS: Officer Candidate School (Navy/Marine/Army) School for college graduates to train to enter the service

OTS: Officer Training School (Air Force) School for college graduates to train to enter the service

PCS: Permanent Change of Station

PJ: Parachute Jumper

POV: Personally Owned Vehicle

PX: Post Exchange-Army idea of a department store

ROTC: Reserve Officer Training Corps-College based training program for entrance into the military services

SAMMC: San Antonio Military Medical Center (formerly Brooks Army Medical Center or BAMC)

TDY: Temporary Duty

CHAPTER ONE

Jethro Francis Thomas deserved a freaking medal for suffering during battle and not taking his just rewards. It wasn't the first time he'd had to administer care to a drunken woman, but this one was more than a handful. Elena Santini had the reflexes of a jaguar, even as drunk as she was. There was no doubt in his mind that she was a world class Marine trained to handle adverse conditions. Usually, that made him admire her. Tonight, it was very difficult to remember she was his best friend's sister.

"Hey, we're at my apartment!"

He looked at her to see if she was messing with him. She frowned in the direction of her apartment building, then looked at him. Damn, he couldn't really tell. It was always hard to tell with her. From the time she was a kid, Elena had to think on her feet. JT knew that Elena had a hard time keeping up with her five brothers. At times, though, she appeared to exceed them. It was always as if Elena seemed to come out on top due to something in her nature. Many people called it being pushy. JT knew it was just part of being a Santini.

"You asked me to bring you here."

She looked at him for a long second. He lost his train

of thought. It had been happening more and more these last few years. Since the year she turned twenty-one. It was her birthday and, with a little too much wine in her system, she had leaned over and gave him a big, sloppy kiss.

It had shattered his world.

They were surrounded by her family and friends, which included his best friend. He could still remember the feel of her mouth against his. She had let him go and gone on her way as if she'd kissed one of her brothers. He'd been standing there painfully aroused and feeling like scum.

"I asked you to take me home."

Okay, maybe she was really drunk. "Yes. So I did."

She pursed her lips and looked around. He fought the need to reach out and touch her long golden brown curls. They were so silky soft he could just imagine the feel of them against his bare flesh.

When she turned back to him, her eyebrows were lowered in confusion.

"This isn't your apartment."

Yep, she was drunk. He decided not to debate the point. Elena could argue with a fence post when she was sober. She was worse with a drink or two in her. All the Santinis were. They all had over the top personalities that were enhanced by alcohol.

"I'll come around."

He slipped out of his truck and rounded the hood. JT decided to take his time to cool his hormones. Elena didn't know what she was doing to him. It was enough that *that* memory kept rearing its ugly head now that she was stationed at Miramar.

Dealing with a tipsy Elena was asking him a bit much. He'd wanted to touch her since the moment he saw her in the bar and grill.

I'll take her to her apartment. Then, go home.

But he didn't want to do that. He wanted to take her inside of her apartment and strip her out of those low riding jeans, taste every bit of her flesh, and lose himself in her.

Dammit.

He didn't need to be contemplating sex with Elena. He had other things to worry about. Going back undercover was just part of his job at NCIS, and getting tangled up with a woman was definitely not the thing to do. Especially Elena.

He drew in another deep breath of fresh air before opening the passenger side door. Getting hot over his best friend's little sister was definitely not on his agenda. Anthony would kick JT's ass if he had any idea of the fantasies he'd had about Elena.

That thought was enough to clear his mind and settle his hormones. *Almost.*

Knowing it would be best to get her into her apartment and be on his way, he opened the door. She must have been leaning against the door, because she tumbled out of his pickup and into his arms.

"Whoops," she said, her voice filled with laughter.

And for an instant, he could think of nothing but her wonderful curves pressed up against him. All those worries about Anthony and his job faded away. The very sexy woman in his arms took over his every thought.

She settled her head against his shoulder. Her breath danced over his neck. A shiver of need rushed over him. It took every ounce of his control to set her away from him.

"Your keys," he growled.

She blinked at him. "What?"

"I need your key." He bit out every word. It was that or scream in frustration.

"Are you the Key Master?" she asked, smiling at him. "That would make me the Gatekeeper."

He shook his head and tried to figure out if she was the only one who was drunk. He'd had a few beers, but he didn't even have a buzz anymore. So, it had to be her.

"What the hell are you talking about?"

"You know, Ghostbusters. Key Master and the Gatekeeper."

It was his turn to blink. She was talking about a movie, and he was trying to figure out if she was wearing a bra with a front clasp or not. He was scum. Worse. He was lower than scum.

"I think I need to get you inside."

She snorted.

"What?"

She shook her head and just gave him a smile.

Knowing Elena, it was just better to ignore her and get her inside. From the time he had met her years ago, she had always been smart-mouthed. It had just gotten worse as she had gotten older. Now, it was impossible to control what came out of her mouth.

"Key."

She shrugged and turned around, grabbing her purse. She pulled out a key ring that had more trinkets hanging off it than keys. He shook his head and grabbed it. He guided Elena to her apartment door. It wasn't that simple, of course. She tripped over her own feet, twice. By the time they made it the door, he was convinced she was doing it all on purpose. He set her away from him again. He struggled to slip the key into the doorknob, but it wasn't easy. Elena had slipped her hands around his waist and pressed that amazing body against his back.

JT couldn't fight his reaction. It was impossible. Even knowing that she was off limits, his body didn't give a damn. His blood went from cool to hot in the span of a second.

Her hands dipped down below his belt. He dropped the keys. They clanked on the cement.

"Uh-oh," she said, then she snorted. "I thought you were supposed to be good with your hands.

He turned around and found her so close he had to back up a step. Unfortunately, his head smacked the door he was just trying to unlock. He looked down at her and felt heat pulse through his blood.

Do not lust after your best friend's little sister.

She leaned against him. He could feel her breath against his neck again.

And definitely don't kiss her. No matter how much you want to.

"Jethro, Jethro." She giggled again.

He hadn't heard her giggle this much since the first day he met her. When she had been a girl. *Jesus.* He had actually known her before she could wear a bra.

"Does anyone say anything about you being an NCIS agent with the first name of Jethro?"

It wasn't easy having a name of the head agent of the popular TV series. In fact, it made it harder to get respect many times. "All the time."

He took her by the arms and set her away from him. Turning, he grabbed the keys, and unlocked the door finally. Opening the door, he stepped aside and let her walk by him. She did, and immediately tripped over the threshold. He caught her before she could fall face first on the foyer.

He righted her again, but she stepped closer and leaned against him. The clean, wild scent of her surrounded him…tempted him.

Holy Mother of God.

She was slithering against him again. She wrapped her arms around his neck. Before he could react, she planted a wet, sloppy kiss on his mouth. He responded to it before he could think. She slipped her tongue between his lips, and he was lost for a few moments. He could think of nothing else than the taste of her mouth, the texture of her lips.

Finally, he remembered who she was, who he was, and how wrong it all was. He pulled away but she tried to follow him, her lips pursed, her eyes closed.

"No."

"Yes," she said, her eyes still closed.

Her mouth turned down in a frown, and her eyes

fluttered open. God, she was gorgeous. She always had been pretty, but now that she had matured and added a little meat on her bones, she was stunning. The fact that he knew the inside was even more beautiful made her damned difficult to resist.

"No. You are Anthony's sister."

She furrowed her brow. "So?"

He sighed. "Guys don't mess with their best friend's little sisters."

"I'm not little."

"But you *are* Anthony's younger sister. I can't step over that line."

She studied him for a second or two. Then, he realized her eyes were clear. She wasn't as tipsy as she had him believe earlier. She was always good at playing a role to get what she wanted.

"So, you can't step over the line, but you kiss like you want to."

Dammit, the woman was always straightforward. It was something he loved about her, most of the time. When she had that perception zeroed in on him, though, he didn't like it one bit. JT knew his limits and if he didn't get out of there, he would make a very big mistake.

"I didn't think. I just reacted."

It sounded lame because it *was* lame. Something passed over her expression that looked like disappointment.

She sighed. "Okay. See ya around."

She turned away from him and he felt…deflated. It was the only thing that could describe the feeling that now morphed his better judgment. He knew he should go, but something nagged at him.

"That's it?"

She looked him, her face expressionless.

"What do you want me to say? Stay safe and call us when you get back?"

"It might be a few months." She nodded in response, then he realized what she said. "Us?"

"Yes. Dante. I'm including him."

She said nothing else and it irritated him. Seriously? The woman who had kissed him like she needed the kiss more than she needed her next breath was just sending him off with a 'see ya'?

"What's the matter, Jethro? Expected me to beg?" she asked, sarcasm dripping from every word.

"No." Not really. "I just expected…"

"Listen, you might think of me as a little girl, but I'm a grown up. You don't have the courage to face your attraction head on. I can deal with that. Doesn't mean I'm going to sit around hoping some day you will get over it. I might want you, but it doesn't mean I'm going to wait for you to grow a set of balls."

His pride took the direct hit. He didn't like it one bit. He was the one ready to make the sacrifice. "Hey!"

She shrugged. "Now, I just want to go to sleep."

He knew she was screwing with him. Growing up with five brothers had given Elena a good idea on how to handle men. She'd had most of her brothers dancing to her tune for years.

"You want me to leave?"

"Yes."

It was his turn to blink. "Just like that?"

She crossed her arms and nodded. "Just like that."

"Well…"

She made a sound that was halfway between a growl and a shout.

"Good lord, just go, JT. You made your position clear. I'm a big girl. You would have kissed any woman back who had locked lips with you. Now, could you leave so I can go disinfect my mouth, because you are apparently a whore with your mouth?"

He hesitated, then turned to walk to the door. He stepped up to the threshold, but…he couldn't do anything. No matter what he told himself, he couldn't force himself to take that last step away from her.

Even though he knew he shouldn't do it, he turned and looked at her one last time. She wasn't crying, wasn't smiling. Just nothing. And that told him one thing.

She was lying.

Instead of walking out the door, he slammed it shut and turned to stride in her direction. Her eyes widened as she dropped her hands down to her sides. He slipped his arm around her waist and yanked her against him. She gasped.

"This time, I'll do the kissing," he said.

Before he could have second thoughts, he crushed his mouth down on hers and damned them both.

CHAPTER TWO

For a moment or two, the world seemed to stop. Elena's mind went blank as JT slanted his mouth over hers and deepened the kiss. For a long second, she couldn't respond. It was as if her brain had gone on hiatus. She was so stunned.

Then, in one blinding instant, her hormones took over. Heat rushed over her as a painful craving filled her soul. With a moan, she wrapped her arms around him and leaned in closer. JT slipped his hands down to her ass and urged her closer to him. He was fully erect, straining against his jeans. Elena pressed closer. A primal groan erupted from his throat as he pulled back from the kiss. Worried that he might be trying to move away from her, she tried to follow him. Instead, he kissed his way down her neck.

Shivers of need raced over her flesh as he nipped at the delicate skin. Each time she felt his teeth scrape against her throat, it increased the bone deep longing she had for him. Everything in the world melted away. Elena couldn't even think of anything to do. She shuddered as he kissed his way up to her ear and pulled her lobe between his teeth.

Lord have mercy.

JT pulled back, drawing in whole gulps of air. Suddenly, without a word, he grabbed her hand and dragged her behind him. She stumbled over her feet and almost fell down. If he hadn't had a hold of her hand, she would have definitely made a fool out of herself.

"Hey," she said, but he ignored her. He was apparently on a mission of some sort. He tugged her through the doorway then spun her around. With ease, he tumbled them both onto her bed.

She laughed as he bent his head to kiss her mouth. This time, she was ready, but she was still surprised by the rush of desire that enveloped the two of them. Elena wasn't a virgin, but she felt like it. His tongue swept into her mouth and she sighed into the kiss. Slipping her hands up and over his shoulders, she molded her hands to the back of his head. With ease, she tangled her tongue against his, enjoying the way his body jerked at the first touch. He pulled her tongue into his mouth and sucked on it.

Damn.

He tore his mouth away from hers and scooted down the bed. With little finesse, JT shoved her shirt up then tugged it over her head. It was tossed somewhere on the floor beside her bed.

He unsnapped the front clasp of her bra and bent his head. Before she could draw in a breath, he had his mouth on her nipple, teasing it with his tongue and teeth. She slipped her fingers through his hair, and molded her hands to the back of his head again.

The need he had built was almost painful now. Every fiber of her being needed his touch. Every slide of his hand and his tongue pushed her desire to a higher level.

She arched against him, moaning as he grazed his teeth over the tip of her nipple before he kissed his way down her body. He unsnapped her jeans and then tugged them off her, throwing them behind him. She laughed and he stilled. The serious look on his face had her heart lodging somewhere in her throat. It took considerable effort to swallow and gain her voice.

"What?" she asked, even though she was afraid of the answer.

"I just…" He sighed.

Her worry escalated. If he backed out now, she just might die. No, first she would kill him, then she would die.

His mouth slowly curved and his eyes heated. "I love the way you sound when you laugh."

She blinked as something shifted in her chest. Why did she feel like crying all of a sudden? Men didn't try to romance her, and she avoided it most of the time. Romance meant attachment, and she had never really wanted that. *Before now.*

Dammit, why did he have to say such sweet things to her? It was going to be hard to deal with the memories without also remembering the things he said to her.

"Yeah?"

He nodded, then his smile turned into a grin. Her heart lodged in her throat, and she found it hard to catch her breath. Damn, he went from adorable to downright sexy in a split second.

"I like it as much as I liked hearing you moan my name."

He kept his gaze locked with hers, as he slipped her panties down her legs. Settling back on top of her, he started to drive her insane. His hands and his mouth moved over her flesh, tempting her, overwhelming her. He slicked his tongue over one of her nipples, as he pinched and teased the other one.

She moved against him and moaned again. She couldn't help it. The rough fabric of his jeans added another level of frustration to the need he was building inside of her. Her sex was damp, and he had barely touched her. She knew this was just the beginning of what would probably be the best sex of her life.

He chuckled as he kissed his way down her stomach. He grazed his teeth over her belly button and she looked down at him. He looked at her, his gaze locked on hers as he moved further down. Once he settled between her legs, he placed a kiss on each of her inner thighs before she felt his breath against her sex. He gave her little time to prepare before he set his mouth against her.

She gasped as he slid his tongue inside of her, then up over her clit. With each lick, he pushed her closer and closer to the edge of pleasure, but did not allow her to fall. She closed her eyes and moaned his name. Or something. She wasn't sure what she was saying at the moment; because he was pushing every sensual button she seemed to have on her body. He slid a finger inside, as he teased the little bundle of nerves with his teeth. Over and over he tormented her with his mouth, his fingers, and his teeth. When she thought she couldn't take it anymore, her orgasm washed over her, through her. Everything in the world faded away and gratification consumed her.

She was still in a haze as he slid off the bed and out of his clothes. Damn. JT wasn't big and bulky. He was lean, sculpted, as if an artist had chiseled him out of stone.

Years ago, she remembered being struck dumb when she saw him in his swimming trunks. But the years had been kind to the very special agent Thomas. A spattering of hair covered his chest, thinning to a line that traveled all the way down his stomach, bisecting an amazing set of abs. His erection curved up against his abdomen.

By the time she could think straight again, he was already grabbing a condom and returning to the bed. Elena reached out, trying to wrap her hand around his cock, but he swatted it away.

"Hey," she said, irritated that he was denying her.

JT shook his head and offered her a rueful smile. "No. I want to actually make it inside of you before I embarrass myself."

Elena wanted to argue, but then, how could a woman be irritated with a man who said things like that? Add on the way her body was still on a high from the orgasm he just gave her, Elena couldn't complain. He rolled the condom on and kneeled between her legs. He took her hips in his hands and, keeping his gaze locked with hers, he thrust into her. She was still sensitive from her orgasm, but she felt too damned good to care. Having him inside her felt right...and complete.

He rested his forehead against hers and started to move. He kept his gaze locked with her as he thrust in and out of her. Elena considered herself an experienced lover, but never in her life had a man overwhelmed her. It wasn't just because she loved him…it was the way he made love to her. The heat in his eyes flushed through her blood. He was shaking with his need for release but he didn't rush. Slowly, easily, he started to build her up to another orgasm. Every nerve ending in her body seemed to be lit on fire, ready to explode.

Elena wrapped her legs around his waist as he continued moving, his thrusts speeding up.

He bent down and kissed her, slipping his tongue between her lips. Whispering, he said, "Come with me, Elena. Be with me."

She couldn't resist the request. She arched against him as her orgasm rushed through her.

He moaned her name over and over, following her into oblivion. Long moments later, he collapsed on top of her. Elena wrapped her arms around him, hugging him close.

In that one moment, she knew she would never be the same again, but she couldn't regret it. Not now. Not ever. Tasting heaven, even for one night, was worth a lifetime of heartache.

CHAPTER THREE

JT settled back against the pillows and wrapped his arm around Elena. Satiated—for the moment—he wanted to enjoy this moment as much as the sex. She snuggled close to him, apparently in no hurry to get up or get dressed. Her head was on his shoulder, and her hand rested on his chest—right over his heart. The scent of their lovemaking tinted the air, but there was something more there. He could smell her on her sheets. She wasn't a woman who wore perfume. Instead, he could smell her lotion and shampoo, along with the sensual musk that clung to her. He trailed his fingers over her upper arm, enjoying the silky feel of her skin. JT knew that he would be happy to spend a week or more in bed with her. Just like this.

He knew that this wasn't just for one night.

He waited for the panic to set in. Touching her had been something he'd been avoiding for a couple of years. Was it because he had known it would be like this? He'd ended an engagement over his feelings. It wasn't that he thought he would ever act on them, but he couldn't marry Bethany if he could be that attracted to Elena. He thought it had just been something lacking in the relationship. For Bethany, he knew she had been having second thoughts about being married to an NCIS agent. It was exciting for her in the beginning, but his long hours had dimmed that excitement. Arguments led to tears and then, by the time he called it off, Bethany had seemed almost bored. That was not what he wanted in a marriage.

He had always had a picture-perfect idea of marriage. He didn't get the idea from his own house. His parents didn't have a good marriage. His father was an abusive prick, and until he met the Santinis, JT had no idea that married couples actually acted in a loving way together. A touch, a smile…just a small gesture was all it took for the Santinis to know how loved they were. He wanted something like that. Long-standing, loving, and unable to keep his hands off his wife, even after twenty years of marriage.

He rubbed his chin on top of Elena's head. JT wasn't too sure she was going to agree with him. He knew she cared for him. While Elena might have an adrenaline junkie kind of job, she didn't take risks in her personal life. She wouldn't take a chance on something like this. Still, he wasn't sure what she expected out of it. JT knew what he wanted, but he was also older.

Eventually, he would have to deal with Anthony and how they would go on with their friendship. The ramifications of their lovemaking could bring an end to the relationship he had with Anthony. From the moment they'd met, they had been as close as brothers. Now, he didn't know if Anthony would talk to him again once he found out. *Damn.*

"Lord, stop thinking." Her husky voice filtered over him. Even though she was telling him what to do, he couldn't help but enjoy listening He could wake up hearing that voice for the rest of his life.

He shook that feeling away. He couldn't deal with that thought tonight. If he thought about it too much, he would definitely do something stupid…like tell Elena.

JT looked down at her. She still had her head against his chest. Her curls caught on the stubble on his chin.

"What?"

"You're thinking about things. No good can come of that."

There was something to be said about sleeping with a woman who had known him probably close to half his life. She knew him a little too well for him to lie. It was going to make the intricacies of dating a little bit more difficult.

"There are issues we have to talk about."

She sighed. "Why do we have to talk about it?"

"Elena, we can't pretend that we didn't just make love."

She pulled away from him and sat up, pulling up the sheet to cover her breasts—unfortunately. He had to curl his fingers into the sheet to keep from grabbing the fabric and tugging it down. He hadn't gotten to see enough of her naked. He was pretty sure he would never get enough of seeing her naked. But this was important.

There was little light in the room, but the living room light spilled into the bedroom through the door. There was enough to allow him a good view. She might be hiding the most important parts, but damn, he couldn't complain. Her hair was tousled and her lips still swollen from his kisses.

"JT, I knew going into this that it would only be tonight. When are you leaving? Tomorrow? Monday?"

"Monday."

"And when will you be back?" she asked in a knowing tone.

He didn't know. This one was going to be deeper than the last few, and it could be weeks before he returned. He reached out and played with the ends of her hair. She had always kept it long, but it was probably longer than she had ever had it since he had known her. The bangs she'd added set off her amazing eyes. It felt like silk. He knew a lot of people used that term to describe hair, but it was the only thing that came to mind.

"You don't know, do you?" she asked.

He studied her expression for a moment. One thing about Elena was that she didn't like liars. In fact, she couldn't stand them. She was always straight up honest with everyone, which was one reason she didn't have a lot of female friends. He was sure growing up with five Santini brothers had something to do with that personality trait.

He shook his head as he took her hand in his. "Not really. It's going to be deep."

She studied their joined hands for a moment, then looked up at him. "I would love to take this further, but we have to wait. Starting things up would make it more complicated and much worse when you leave. Don't you see that?"

He nodded, even if he didn't like it. She was right. "I know that both of us have a lot on our plates."

"And neither of us can say what the future holds right now. If you weren't leaving, then I'd probably call in sick and not leave bed for a week."

But he wanted a commitment. "I just wonder what your brothers will say about it."

"Why would they say anything about it? How are they going to know?"

"When I'm involved with a woman, I don't hide it."

Although, he couldn't remember the last time he'd had that kind of relationship. His job had made it difficult and since his engagement dissolved, he just hadn't taken the time to really date. This was different though. "Do we really need that complication? We have no reason to tell anyone."

"Why?"

"Why what?"

He fought the need to growl at her. He knew she wasn't being deliberately obtuse. "Why can't we tell anyone?"

JT knew he was getting irritated, and he really didn't understand why. He knew it had to do with the fact that she didn't want to tell anyone about them. He understood to a point, but it just struck him as odd. As the woman, shouldn't she be the one pushing this angle? Most women liked talking about such things. It was one of the reasons he avoided these kind of entanglements in recent years.

"For what? One night of sex?"

He hated the way she said it. She made it sound cheap. "If I wasn't leaving Monday, it would definitely be more than that."

She cocked her head and studied him. Elena was rarely calm or quiet, so when she was, it was always odd. And, as Anthony said more than once, always fear Elena when she was quiet. There was a good chance she was formulating a way to make you cry.

"But you *are* leaving."

"What about when I get back?"

She sighed, the sad sound echoed through him and touched his soul. Never in his life had he wanted to soothe a woman's unhappiness. It was as if she were unhappy, he was too.

"I'm assuming you won't be able to contact anyone?" she asked.

He nodded.

She was quiet for a second, then she looked him straight in the eye. "Why don't we just say you will look me up when you get back? We'll decide on where to go from there."

It was practical, and normally, he should be happy with it. Any other woman said it to him, he would be relieved. Now, the words bothered him. He couldn't put his finger on it, but something was wrong.

"I see you working it out there in your head, Jethro."

He shook his head and she laughed.

"Listen, if you weren't leaving Monday, I would be more than happy to tie you down in more ways than one." She wiggled her sculpted eyebrows. "But, you and I both know this next assignment is going to be long and deep. If we had been dating, that would be one thing."

She was saying all the right things, but it left him with a hollow feeling in the pit of his stomach. When he didn't respond, she leaned forward and brushed her mouth against his.

"Just let us have tonight. We'll worry about the future later."

He wanted more from her. He wanted to demand some kind of agreement, but he knew that wasn't fair to either of them. She was right, even if it hurt his heart to admit it.

So, instead of pushing the issue, he deepened the kiss. He let go of her hand and tugged on the sheet. It slipped down, and she lifted her leg to straddle him. She was already hot and wet. Needing to taste, he rose up and took one hardened nipple into his mouth. She leaned her head back and moaned as he teased her. Her hair was so long, the tips brushed his legs.

She shuddered as he moved his mouth from one nipple to the other. He had never had a woman who was as responsive as she was. He touched her and she exploded. It was as if they were made for each other.

Soon, though, she was pushing him back on the bed. She kissed her way down his torso. Her teeth scraped against his abdomen before she settled between his legs. She wrapped her hand around his cock and gave it one, long, leisurely stroke. He watched as she bent her head over and licked the head. He closed his eyes and groaned as she took him fully into her mouth. Soon he was lifting his hips off the bed to keep rhythm with her. God, it felt good. Too good. He almost lost his control. He didn't want this. He wanted to share, to feel those little muscles of hers contract around his cock as he came.

He pulled her up and she frowned at him. "In a hurry, Jethro?"

He growled and tried to roll them over, but she shook her head.

"Nope, my turn."

She grabbed a condom off her bedside table. She had it on quickly, then rose up over him. Slowly, surely, she took him inside of her. She bent down as she continued to move and kissed him. This wasn't a simple kiss. In it, he felt her need, and the connection he had been missing with every other woman. In that one split second, he knew she was the mirror to his soul.

Pulling away, she sat up. As she continued to move, she leaned her head back and moaned. It was one of the most erotic things he had ever seen. And beautiful. So fucking beautiful.

They moved in rhythm. It was only their second time making love, and it was as if they already understood each other in bed. He slipped his hands on her hips, digging his fingers into her flesh as she continued to ride him. Each time she moved, it heightened his need, drawing him deeper into the web of erotic pleasure she wound around him. Her muscles clenched tightly against his cock—tighter each time she sank onto him. Her moans grew as she moved faster over him. JT slipped his fingers down between them, pressing against her clit, sending her flying over into her orgasm.

She screamed, her body convulsing as all those tiny inner muscles clasped tight against him, drawing him deeper into her hot core.

He rolled them over, switching their positions again and started to thrust hard and deep inside of her. He was mindless to anything but their pleasure. As he felt his own orgasm approaching, Elena came again beneath him, arching up against him and moaning his name. In that last instant, he joined her, gaining his pleasure as he groaned her name against her lips.

CHAPTER FOUR

The sun was peeking through the blinds as Elena stirred awake. It was warm and comfy in her bed and a weekend day. She rarely slept passed sunrise on duty days. Now that she had a hot NCIS agent in her bed, she definitely didn't see a reason to get out of bed.

With JT on her mind, she rolled over and reached for him. Unfortunately, she found the bed empty. She opened her eyes and looked around. At first, she thought JT had left. There was a stillness in the room. Something cold shifted in her chest and it almost hurt. JT did have a reputation with woman, and he tended to disappear from what she'd heard. She noticed his shirt laying on the chair beside her bed, but not jeans. She listened carefully and heard movement in the kitchen.

Elena slipped out of bed and snatched up his shirt on the way to the bathroom. After taking care of her pressing needs, she slipped the shirt on over her head. She pulled on a pair of panties, then went in search of JT.

She found him in the kitchen drinking coffee and looking out the window. He wasn't wearing anything but a pair of jeans that hung low on his hips. Lord have mercy, the man was a god of golden skin and muscles.

Elena still couldn't believe he was there. For years she had been attracted to him. It wasn't easy gaining the attention of her oldest brother's best friend. Especially when that friend had known her since she was twelve. She had flirted a little, and he had practically patted her on the head. She had almost given up, and probably would have if she hadn't run into him and Dante the night before. With a little liquid courage, she had taken a chance.

JT must have sensed her presence, because he turned his head and looked at her.

Damn. Those amazing gray eyes always seemed to see more than other people. She was sure it was one of the things that made him good at his job as an NCIS agent. The silence stretched between them, and she had to fight the need to shift her feet.

"Morning," she said, feeling suddenly shy.

Elena wasn't someone who usually had problems with the morning afters. She didn't sleep around, but she also wasn't ashamed to have a sex life. Her mother had raised her to have a healthy view of sex. Of course, she couldn't really remember a man looking at her the way JT was looking at her now. He was watching her like a predator. One that wanted to take a big, juicy bite out of her.

"Morning, Elena," he said, his mouth curving up on one side.

Oh, boy.

She couldn't speak. For a long moment, she stood there not able to even move. Her heart beat hard against her chest, as her brain went amazingly blank. His gaze dipped down her body then back up. Her body flushed with heat. She felt awkward the longer he stared at her. Mentally, she shook herself and smiled.

"Amazing sex and coffee in the morning?" She walked to the counter to grab a coffee cup and fill it up. "I might just have to keep you around."

Before she could turn around, he stepped up behind

her and slipped his arm around her waist.

"I was hoping for more than one night, though."

She closed her eyes and tried to compose herself. Elena had such a crush on this man for so long, she really didn't know what to say to him now. She knew it wasn't just the exciting feelings of a schoolgirl. *Love.* She did love him, and it scared the living hell out of her. But, she couldn't deal with that right now. And she couldn't make him deal with it. His next assignment was going to be probably the most dangerous of his career. He didn't need baggage from her to worry about.

She turned around and was surprised to see the earnest expression on his face. He wasn't flirting; he was serious.

"JT," she said, setting her coffee on the counter then cupping his face. "I would love to say we will have a future, but we talked about that last night."

He nodded. "Yes, and I can handle that. Sort of. And I have things to do. I hate to leave like this."

She nodded. "I understand."

"I wish we had more time together."

She smiled. "We'll have time when you get back."

Something close to relief filtered over his expression. "Yeah?"

Her heart squeezed tight. She knew that the request hadn't been easy to make. You didn't grow up in a house with five brothers and not understand how their minds worked. Pride was more important to them than the air they needed to live. She leaned forward and brushed her mouth over his, then pulled back.

"I need to go get my car from Madison's house."

He nodded. "I can take you, then I need to go in and do a few things for work."

She nodded. "I guess we better get our butts in gear."

"Not until I have a proper good morning kiss."

The way his voice moved over the syllables had her toes curling against the linoleum.

"Is that a fact?"

He nodded as he bent his head. She rose up on her toes to meet him halfway, unable to wait. The moment their mouths touched, she felt need explode within her. Heat coursed through her veins as he deepened the kiss. By the time he lifted his head, they were both breathing heavily.

"I need to take a shower."

He set his coffee cup next to hers. "Imagine that."

"What?"

"So do I."

Her brain just stopped working right then. It was as if it had melted somewhere along the way. Then, she laughed and slipped away from him. She turned and walked backward.

"I'll share…only if you catch me."

His eyes darkened and she turned to run. He easily caught up with her and picked her up, slinging her over his shoulder.

"Jethro put me down."

"Nope," he said, smacking her rear end.

He made his way to the bathroom, then set her down on the floor. He kept her close against his body, and it was hard to miss the erection straining against the denim.

"Elena."

She barely heard him whisper her name. Her heart trembled, then tumbled down. Oh, god, she was going to hurt so much when he left. It was going to feel worse than going unnoticed. Now she knew what it was like to lay beside him in bed and feel him there next to her.

He leaned down and took her mouth in a sweet kiss, one that did more to overwhelm her than anything he had ever done before. It was soft and wet and she felt it down to the bottom of her feet.

When he pulled back, she blinked trying to stem the flood of tears that threatened to embarrass her.

"What?" he asked.

She shook her head, then smiled. "I think you earned a shower with me, very special agent Jethro Thomas."

He made a face as she walked over to start the shower. It always took it a while to heat up.

"Do me a favor?"

She looked back over her shoulder. "What?"

"Stop calling me Jethro Thomas."

She laughed. "If you promise to scrub my back."

He grabbed her and pulled her closer, turning her so she could face him. "I promise to do a lot more than that in the shower."

She ignored the anxiety that was clenching her stomach and kissed him. She'd worry about missing him tomorrow.

* * * *

Elena glanced at the clock beside her bed. Three A.M. It was always bad when she got insomnia. Usually, she would get up and work out, or maybe do some other kind of busy work. She didn't feel like it.

After leaving her brother and Madison, she had been unsettled. She wished it had to do with what had happened. It's not every day your friend sees a murder and your brother's house gets trashed. Guilt flitted through her, but she ignored it. Elena knew she couldn't help but worry about JT.

He was going to leave on Monday morning, and he would be gone for a few weeks, maybe even months. She didn't know exactly what this was about, but she knew it was important enough for him to go right back under. Since Anthony was an agent also, she knew they rarely went back into undercover work without a little down time. Even knowing it was a strain on him, JT had volunteered. She admired him for that. Santinis always served in some capacity, and since he was considered an honorary Santini, she knew it was in his blood to serve too. She just didn't expect it to be so hard.

She was in love with him.

She had thought the words before, but now she was

being hit over the head with it. It was killing her not knowing when she would see him again. He was going into a dangerous situation; she knew that for sure. And she would have to wait for a call from Anthony if JT did get hurt.

Her cell phone buzzed, and she looked at the display.

JT.

She drew in a deep breath and answered.

"Did I wake you?"

She closed her eyes and tried not to let her emotions take over. Elena knew she was pretty close to begging him to come to her apartment.

"No. I was up."

"I've been up all night."

Opening her eyes, she frowned up at the ceiling. "That's not good. You need your sleep."

"Yeah. But, then, I wanted to see you."

"I'd love that too, but I assumed you had work to get out of the way."

"I did. I'm all ready. Bags packed, everything ready for an extended absence."

"Hmmm, but you still can't sleep? I could help with that."

"I'm pretty sure you could. In fact, that's what is keeping me up."

"Really?" she asked, her heart doing a little jig. The fact that he was thinking about her too boded well for when he got back.

"Yeah. I can't stop thinking about the way you taste."

She couldn't talk. Air tangled in her throat, rendering her almost speechless. Heat raced over her nerve endings. Her heart was pounding so hard against her chest, Elena was surprised he couldn't hear it over the phone.

"I especially like hearing you moan my name."

She closed her eyes and tried to get her hormones under control. She loved when he said that to her. "You really shouldn't call me and say things like that. It's not fair."

"Well, I guess that's good then."

"Why?"

"I'm standing outside your door."

She sat up. "My door? At my apartment?"

"Yes."

She jumped out of bed and made her way there. "Why?"

She opened the door before he could answer. He was standing there, holding his phone and looking too delicious to ignore.

He turned off his phone. "I had to see you."

Without a word, she grabbed his hand and yanked him into her apartment. He kissed her, slamming the door shut with his foot and fumbling with the lock as she tore at his clothes. He didn't let her finish right there. Instead, he pulled back and pulled her up into his arms.

"We only have a few hours," he said, his voice deep with need.

She kissed his neck. "So what are you waiting for?"

He laughed and made his way back to her bedroom. "I like a woman who knows what she wants."

"Then you're going to *love* me."

He threw her onto the bed, and ccvered her body with his. And neither of them talked about anything else for quite some time.

CHAPTER FIVE

The next morning, JT was worried. Not about the mission, which was a whole other batch of worries. He was concerned about the woman sitting beside him.

She'd been quiet since they'd had breakfast. It was an air of pensive thought that filled the apartment, and he wondered if she was having second thoughts.

When he had suggested a movie, something they had both seen before, she'd agreed. Now, though, he thought maybe he should have kept her busy. In the quiet times, he could almost hear her thinking.

"What's got you so quiet?"

She glanced at him then back to the TV.

"I have a lot on my mind."

That didn't sound good. Elena rarely was so quiet.

"Having second thoughts?" he asked.

She shook her head.

"Elena."

She turned and focused on him. "I'm not really. It's just that stuff with Madison and Dante. It's a lot to handle for people in normal situation, but Mad has made so much progress. I would hate to think this would derail that." She sighed. "Plus, I'm trying to figure out what the hell is going on between Mad and Dante."

"Yeah, I got a vibe from them too."

"He's always had a thing for her. He just never admitted it to anyone, especially himself."

He nodded and grabbed some more popcorn. "He knows about us."

She slanted him a look and took some popcorn too. That was somewhat better. Not much got in the way of Elena and food. When she showed little interest in one of her favorite snacks, he'd wondered about it.

"He didn't say anything, did he?"

His mind went back to the discussion they'd had at Dante's house. "Just that he knew about us. I guess I should have gotten another shirt. He did say to be wary of your brothers."

"He better have not warned you off me. He will be very sorry if he does. Or, if he tells the others. World of pain kind of trouble. "

He watched as she turned back to the movie. There was something in her tone that clicked. "You have blackmail."

She snorted as she slanted him a look out of the corner of her eye. "Well, if you swear not to reveal what I know…"

He crossed his heart. "Swear."

She laughed and turned to face him. "See, when Dad was stationed at the Pentagon—"

"When you two were in high school?"

She nodded. "We were actually living close to Quantico. Dad had a long drive, but they wanted to keep us sort of in a normal area. Anyway, there was this O-6 at Quantico who had this horribly trashy daughter."

"Really?"

She shook her head. "No one really knew it. She acted like some kind of saint when adults were around, but she went after every abled-bodied guy in the vicinity when out on her own."

Again he studied her. "This sounds personal."

"Damn right it is. She slept with Roger."

"Who's Roger?"

"He was supposed to be my prom date."

"When was this?"

"My freshman year."

"You had a prom date your freshman year?"

"Yeah."

"I don't remember that."

She rolled her eyes. "I doubt very much you were paying much attention to Anthony's little sister at that point."

"That's true."

"Anyway, she set her sights on Dante. And, even knowing it was going to be a problem, he slept with her."

He shrugged. "Oh, is that all? I thought it was something bad."

She rolled her eyes. "You are just like all those losers I share DNA with, but the blackmail lives on. First, her father was about to become our father's next CO. Add in that he snuck into her house, he knew he would be in so much trouble with Mom and Dad."

"Wait. Dante snuck into an O-6's house?"

She laughed. "Yeah."

"How did you find out?"

"I caught him sneaking back in. You should have seen the look on his face. I thought he was going to pass out. Of course, it means more now than it did then."

"What do you mean?"

"Well, that colonel went on to bigger and better things."

Something tugged at his memory, suddenly it hit him. "Holy shit, your brother bedded General Cassidy's daughter?"

"Yep. I tortured him forever about it."

"She was older than you two."

"Yeah, she was a senior. And I think she was his first."

"He bedded the Commandant of the Marine Corps' daughter."

She laughed. "Not only that. He snuck into the house. I think he broke her heart also, because he realized just how bad it was when Dad told us who his new CO was. He completely broke it off with her. Oh, lord, I think he had a real freak out over that."

JT chuckled. "Dante was always getting in trouble."

She nodded as she munched on some popcorn. "It has been delicious messing with him over it. At that point, he wanted an agreement that we wouldn't intrude in each other's relationships. It's hard on him because you know how all those idiots are, but I have that blackmail."

"You are very scary."

She leaned over the bowl of popcorn and kissed him. "Just remember how scary."

Elena was pulling away, but he cupped her face and kissed her again, this time taking it deeper. She tasted of salt and butter from the popcorn, but also of Elena. It was something he would remember until the day he drew his last breath.

He was just thinking of how to convince her to ignore the movie when his cell vibrated against the table next to the couch. He had to keep it on because of work. She sighed and slipped away.

"Go ahead."

One thing about Elena was that she understood about work. He looked at the number and inwardly winced. Anthony.

"It's your brother."

"You know him. Answer it or he won't quit trying. He probably knows about the UA."

She gave him another quick kiss, and left him alone.

He answered. "Hey, Anthony."

"Hey back. Where have you been?" he asked.

"What do you mean?"

"I've been trying to get hold of you since yesterday."

Damn. He forgot about the calls he had missed.

"I've been kind of busy getting ready." And the moment he said the words, guilt tightened his stomach. Damn, he hated lying to Anthony, but he had to respect Elena's wishes—for now.

"Yeah? Well, maybe you should think to call your best friend before going UA."

"I was going to call tonight." Maybe.

"Sure. Anyway, just wanted to tell you to keep your ass in one piece. My mom also said to be careful. She says you're her favorite son."

Mrs. Santini had adopted him. They all knew his background with his father. Calling Jed Thomas an alcoholic was too good of a label for the bastard. He cut ties with his father the moment he graduated from high school, and he didn't even know where he was. From that point on, Mrs. Santini had treated him as one of her kids.

Great, more guilt. He was probably going to have an ulcer by the time he told everyone in her family.

"I went out with Dante the other night. Had a couple of beers and ran into your sister and one of her friends. Seems there's something going on with him and a new woman."

"Huh. Well, I just wanted to make sure I was still on the call list."

Meaning if anything went wrong, Anthony would be called.

"Of course." Until Friday night, he didn't have anyone who needed to know other than the Santinis. Granted, Elena was a Santini, but this was different. He wanted her on the list—and he wanted to be on hers.

He pushed those thoughts away and tried to concentrate on the conversation, because Anthony was still talking.

"Good. I wish you could have found some time to come out here when you got back."

"Yeah, that would have been nice."

Then something caught his attention out of the corner of his eye. Elena was standing in the doorway wearing nothing but a shirt. It skimmed the tops of her thighs, but he had a feeling she didn't have any panties on beneath it. The mischievous smile that curved her lips hit him square in the chest. Damn, the woman was a goddess.

"So, do you know how long?" Anthony asked.

She walked toward him. With each step the shirt moved, but not enough to let him see more. When he looked up at her face, he saw her eyes dancing with amusement. She knew just what she was doing to him and enjoyed it. There was something so damned sexy about a woman who knew how desirable she was. Layer that with a confidence in what she did for a living…in the way she held herself, she was irresistible.

"JT?" Anthony said.

"Sorry, what did you ask?" JT said, trying to keep his breathing under control. Of course, at the moment, he wasn't sure his heart was still beating.

Elena pulled the shirt up and straddled his lap. Well, hell, she definitely wasn't wearing any panties.

"How long?"

"How long what?"

There was silence on the other side of the "Are you sure you're okay for another trip so fast?"

Elena settled on top of him. He could feel the heat of her through his jeans. Then, she moved her hips.

Holy Mother of the sweet baby Jesus. She was going to kill him. He almost dropped the phone, as most of the blood in his brain drained and headed south to his groin.

"Huh, not sure how long."

"Well, get some rest and call me when you can."

"You got it."

He hung the phone up before Anthony could respond. Elena was laughing. He grabbed her face and gave her a long, wet kiss. Then, he lifted them both off the couch.

"Where are you going, Jethro?" she asked as she

wrapped her legs around his waist.

"I'm going to show you what happens to a woman who does naughty things to me when I am talking on the phone."

Elena laughed as he marched them both into the bedroom.

* * * *

As Elena walked JT to the door, she physically hurt thinking of him in danger. She wanted to beg him to stay. But she couldn't. She would not do that to him. His job was such a part of him. It was something she understood. Every Santini did.

He stood in the doorway and slipped his hands around her waist. Bending his head, he took her mouth in a sweet, hot, wet kiss. She shivered as emotions rushed through her. She pushed them down, especially the one that was telling her to cry. She would *not* cry.

He pulled back then rested his forehead on hers. "I wish I had never said I would go back under."

"Don't say that. It would have bugged you."

"How do you know that?"

"I know you, JT. Whatever you are about to go work on is something you've been committed to for awhile."

"Too smart for your own good," he said, shaking his head. There was no heat in the words.

"Can you tell me what time you're heading out?"

"Seven."

She wanted to tell him how she felt. The idea of being separated like this was going to hurt so much, but she couldn't put that on him. It would play with his head, and he needed to have his thoughts in order for the job. That would get him back safe.

"If something happens, Anthony will be called."

She didn't need to ask why his parents wouldn't be first on the list. He rarely talked to them these days.

She nodded and gave him another kiss, knowing this was the last one for a long time.

When he pulled back this time, she let him go. "Be careful."

He nodded. "You be careful yourself, Elena."

He turned to leave, and she watched him until he got into his truck. As his taillights disappeared into the night, she shut the door.

She didn't move. Numbness stole over her. It was as if she was shell-shocked. She didn't know what to do with herself. She was already thinking about him, about the danger he had just walked into. She couldn't ask him not to do it any more than he could ask her not to fly her plane. But, damn, she had wanted to. More than anything else, she wanted to chase after his stupid truck and beg him to stay.

That was not an option.

Then it struck her. A bath would be perfect.

She headed into the bathroom and started up the water. As soon as it was hot enough, she poured in the bubble bath. She grabbed and lit a few candles she had sitting on the counter, carrying a couple with her to the tub. After undressing, she stepped into the tub. She was more than a little sore from her weekend activities with JT. She wasn't a virgin, but she definitely didn't sleep around. It had been a long time since she'd been in a relationship, and her body wasn't accustomed to the kind of lovemaking JT was into.

Just thinking his name, she smiled. Then it faded as she noticed her vision wavered. Shit. Fear hit first. His job was always dangerous, but this one was going to be more hazardous than usual. She closed her eyes and tried to get her emotions under control. Immediately, the visions of him in her bed, and the way he had smiled at her materialized. Not seeing him for weeks on end had never been a problem before, but now…

A sob escaped before she could stop it. Elena couldn't fight it anymore. She leaned her head back on the bath pillow and let the tears flow.

Sometimes crying was the only thing a strong woman could do to keep herself together.

CHAPTER SIX

Elena loved all of her brothers. There was something about each one of them that she admired. They were good men, and they had always had her back. But, they all seemed to know how to get on her nerves. At the moment, Brando, the oldest of the other set of twins, was acting in a way that ensured him pain. Lots of it. She was pretty sure he would end up with broken bones if he did not shut the hell up. From the moment he showed up about a week ago, he had been a complete pain in the butt.

"What do you mean, you don't want to go out tonight?" he asked, irritation easy to hear in his voice. If she didn't know better, she would think he was the younger of the two of them. Of course, Brando had always been hyperactive.

Patience, she reminded herself. It was a freaking, fraking virtue. Or so they said. She usually had no problem keeping her cool, but Brando had been driving her crazy for days.

"I have an early morning tomorrow for work. Anyway, I took you out the last three nights."

He made a sound of disgust but said nothing. He had been acting as if she were his personal social director since he'd arrived. When Brand got restless, he was avoiding something that was bothering him.

Of course, he was the last of several visits from her brothers. The only ones she hadn't seen were Nando, who just PCS'd to Germany, and Anthony, as he lived in Hawaii. And, truthfully, she wouldn't put it past Anthony to show up unannounced. It was his way. Worse, Carlos could show up again and talk about taking her horseback riding. How the hell did they end up with a freaking Santini cowboy in the mix?

Since Dante's wedding, there had been phone calls, sudden appearances, and the worst one yet, a call from her Aunt Joey. The woman could have interrogated the most egregious enemy and gotten what she wanted without raising a hand. True, since JT had left, she had lost weight. Part of that had been worry about him, but she was always dealing with new stress at work. Colonel Vent wasn't really thrilled to be dealing with female pilots. He hadn't harassed her, and he wasn't that bad of a commander. It was just hard to work for a man who didn't like you.

Unfortunately, Brando wasn't done arguing with her. "I'm older than you. You should be partying."

She rolled her eyes and was happy he couldn't see her reaction. Since he'd shown up, he'd been dragging her around. She was too tired to even think about going out to a rowdy bar. Her three in the morning wakeup added to her decision.

"I've never been that much of a partier." That was partly true. She hadn't really partied since the night she and JT had spent together. Even at Madison's bachelorette party, she had been subdued. It was hard to have too big of a party. It was her, Madison, and, *just found out she was pregnant*, Hannah Johnson. "I also have to fly tomorrow. I never do that hung over. Go by yourself or call Dante."

"I can't go by myself. I can't drink and drive. Dante is too caught up in being married to want to go out. He said last night was the last time he would go."

Brando said it as if he couldn't understand why anyone would want to stay in and spend time with his wife. It probably was a foreign concept to him. The man would never settle down.

She stirred the sweet and sour sauce and looked at the meatballs in the oven. The rice was sitting warm in the cooker, and the broccoli was steamed. A couple more minutes and they could eat. She glanced at him and knew he wasn't done arguing. *Damn.*

"I think—"

Her doorbell stopped him in midsentence. Elena thanked the good lord for the interruption.

"Expecting someone?" he asked.

She shook her head. Whoever it was, she would be happy to kiss them. When Brando got a hold of an idea, he would not let it go. Their father said that Brando could argue with a door.

Brando sipped at his beer and walked to the door. He opened it and laughed. She leaned around the corner and almost dropped the spoon. JT was standing there. His expression was so damned comical, and she would have laughed. She couldn't though. It had been months since she had talked to him. She had known he wasn't hurt, or Anthony would have heard.

"The Honorary Santini!" Brando said, giving JT one of his legendary bear hugs, lifting him up off the ground. He set him down, and Brando slung an arm over his shoulder and looked at Elena. "Look who's back from the other side."

She couldn't seem to form words. All she could do was look at him. He'd lost weight. It was the first thing she noticed. His jeans hung low on his hips, his T-shirt looked almost a size too big. He'd had a haircut and shave. Dark circles marred the skin beneath his eyes.

He was staring at her as if he wanted her to say something, but she couldn't think of anything. Her brain seemed to have shut down the moment she saw him.

"Hey, JT." How freaking lame.

He nodded. "Hey, Elena."

His voice deepened over the syllables of her name. It sent heat racing along her flesh, and she had to fight a shiver. She glanced at her brother, who didn't seem to notice.

"I was trying to convince Elena to go out tonight," Brando said. Of course, he hadn't noticed. He was busy sizing up JT. He needed a DD and anyone would do.

"And I said, I have to be at work early in the morning." She looked at JT. "Also, he's leaving out that he's flying out to a boys' week in New Orleans tomorrow. He doesn't really need to go out. He just thinks he needs to go."

There was a beat of silence. JT kept staring at her.

"But, JT's here, and you should want to show him a good time," Brando said. "It's probably been months since he's had some fun."

Another beat of silence. JT's lips twitched. Elena felt her face flush with heat. Lord, she couldn't remember the last time she blushed. She cleared her throat, and JT's smile widened into a grin.

God, she had missed him. She wanted to hit him, but she had missed him like crazy.

"You two can go out," Elena said. Why did she say that? She didn't want JT to go out. She wanted him here, naked, and in her bed.

"We can talk about it," Brando said. "Why don't you eat with us? There's enough for all of us, right, Elena?"

She nodded.

JT smiled. "Been awhile since I've had a home-cooked meal."

She returned his smile. "Good. Grab another plate, Brand."

Brando took off to do her bidding, probably hoping to get JT to go out with him.

"Hope you like sweet and sour meatballs."

JT hummed, low and easy, and just loud enough for

her to hear. "I'll take anything you're offering."

The way he said it told her that he was talking about more than dinner. A moment of silence vibrated between them. She curled her fingers into the palms of her hands, trying her best to resist touching him. Her body warmed as her hormones did a little dance of anticipation.

Neither of them said anything. She couldn't really come up with anything to say, and her apartment was too small. Brando would hear.

Still he stood there, apparently happy to stare at her forever. It took all her control not to fidget.

"You look tired," she said.

"I am. It's been a long couple days of debriefing."

She nodded.

"I would have called."

She shrugged. As a Santini, she understood duty and work. "You couldn't. You were being debriefed."

"Yeah."

Silence again.

"Want a beer?"

He shook his head. "I'll take some water."

"Come on."

He followed her into the kitchen, and she entered just in time to find Brando sticking his finger into the sauce.

"You idiot." She smacked him on the back of the head. "Get out of there. You're going to get burned."

She pushed him out of the way.

"Get JT a bottle of water."

JT smiled. "Nice to know that nothing ever changes with the Santinis."

Brando handed him a bottle. "Yeah. How's that?"

"All of you act like idiots, and Elena is trying to make you act better." He unscrewed the top of the bottle. "I think it's about the same every time you all get together."

"That's true. So, when did you get back?" Brando asked.

Elena needed something to do, so she applied herself

to making dinner. The sooner they ate, the sooner Brando would probably head out for the night. Then, hopefully, she would have JT to herself.

* * * *

JT took a sip of water and tried to be patient. As soon as he had been cleared, he'd headed over to Elena's apartment. He knew he should have called first, but he had been so eager to see her. Controlling his need for her was hard enough, but with Brando there, he was ready to scream. He wanted to touch her. Just a little touch. But he knew if he started, he would probably not be able to stop.

Instead, he leaned against the kitchen counter and watched her work.

Every movement was precise. That was the way it was with Elena. She always had a plan. Right now, she was placing the meatballs in the sauce. God, he had missed her so fucking much.

The assignment had been bad, but he knew he had something to go back to. Every night he had gone to sleep thinking of her, of the way she laughed, the way she looked as she slept, and the way she moaned his name.

Dammit. He had to keep his mind on the topic. When Brando rambled on about things, you never knew where the conversation would end up. Thankfully, Brando's phone rang. He answered and walked down the hall to take the call.

God, he'd missed her, he thought again. Granted, they'd only had two nights together, but it had been the one thing that had kept him going. So many things had gone wrong on the assignment, and he had spent too long undercover. Each week that had passed, he had fallen deeper into the muck.

Elena lifted up on her toes to reach a bowl on the top shelf, and he stepped closer to get it for her. This close he could feel her body heat and smell her shampoo. Also, he smelled her. That unique scent that he would swear he could sense the moment he woke in the morning.

She froze, then shuddered.

"I missed you," JT whispered. "I just didn't know what to do when Brando answered the door."

She nodded. "Don't worry about it."

"I can tell him."

"Tell him what?" she asked, still whispering.

"About us."

She turned and looked up at him. She wasn't wearing any makeup, and this is the way he thought of her. There was nothing plain about the woman…but there was a down to earth quality to her beauty. He knew that fifty years from now she would be just as beautiful. Dark blue eyes were framed with brown lashes, and set off by her bangs. Her full lips and high cheekbones just accentuated her appearance.

"No. Not yet. Seriously, we don't even know what the hell is going to happen, and we don't need my brothers sticking their noses in."

He nodded, barely hearing the words she was saying. All he could think of was that he wanted—*needed*—a taste. This close, he couldn't resist. He leaned down to give her a quick kiss. But the moment he did, he was lost. All that was horrible in the world faded away. The memories of what he had been through dissolved. He slipped his hands down her back and over her full rear end, urging her closer. God, this felt right…good. He had thought of little else the last few months, needing something to keep him going. He wanted nothing more than to take her to bed right then. Fuck dinner. Fuck her brother and anyone else. He needed her with him, like this.

He heard Brando walking down the hall, his voice rising up. "My sister's making dinner, then I can meet you out."

They sprang apart right before Brando turned the corner. He was laughing as he hung up the phone. JT turned away from Brando and grabbed his water. He drained the rest of it in one long swallow. Damn, he had no control whatsoever when it came to Elena.

"What's up?" Elena asked. Her voice was surprisingly calm.

"Got a friend in town. He wants to meet tonight."

"He's here?" Elena asked.

"You know Chet? Remember, you met him at the wedding?"

"Wedding?" JT asked.

Elena smiled. "Madison and Dante."

"Holy shit. They got married?"

She nodded, and it was easy to see her happiness for her friend and twin. "Just a couple of weeks ago. They just returned from their honeymoon. I forget how much you miss while you're gone like that."

He shook his head. "Damn, Little Dante Santini is married."

"This Chet guy is going to go out with you?" Elena asked her brother.

"Don't you remember him? You danced with him."

Elena shook her head and all of a sudden, JT wanted to tear off Chet's arms and beat him over the head with them.

"He's picking you up?" she asked.

Brando nodded.

"Your plan is to get dinner from me, then go party with your friend?" Elena asked.

JT couldn't figure out if she was mad or not about it. Brando just laughed.

"You're sick of me anyway. And this way, Chet and I can drive in his rental to the airport." He looked at JT. "You can come with, if you want to."

He shook his head. "I need to get some sleep before I party. I haven't had much in the last week."

Brando clapped him on the shoulder. "You and Anthony are getting to be old men."

"Dinner's ready," Elena said.

He was ready for this, ready to get Brando out of the apartment, so he and Elena could be alone.

Then, maybe, they could figure out where the hell they went from here.

CHAPTER SEVEN

As soon as the door shut, JT made his way to the kitchen. His fingers were itching to touch her. Hell, his body was humming with the need to feel. Elena was bent over, as she stored the leftovers in the fridge. She straightened just as he came around the corner. JT didn't stop his forward progress until her reached her. He slipped his arm around her waist and yanked her against him. Without hesitation, JT slammed his mouth down on hers. She responded immediately, wrapping her arms around his neck and kissing him back. He ran the tip of his tongue along the seam of her mouth. She opened her mouth, allowing him to slip his tongue inside.

The craving that had been shimmering in his blood from the moment he saw her exploded. It twisted through him, leaving him slightly lightheaded. He could no longer hold back the emotions. He backed her against the counter and lifted her up on it. He needed to touch, to taste.

With hurried movements, he grabbed the bottom of her t-shirt. He pulled back and tugged it over her head, tossing it on the floor behind him. Damn, she wasn't wearing a bra.

He thanked the lord and bent his head to taste. Usually,

he would use more finesse, but he couldn't. It had been months since he had seen her, and he needed her. He knew he would never be able to explain it to anyone, even himself. Something had been missing from his life while he had been away, and it was Elena.

She tugged at his shirt, and he pulled back to let her take it off him. She tossed it behind him and cupped his face in both hands. She kissed him, keeping her eyes opened as she nipped at his lips. He watched as her eyes closed, and she slipped her tongue into his mouth. He closed his eyes and enjoyed the sleek taste of her, and the way her tongue tangled with his.

He was shaking he needed her so badly. He pulled back long enough to help her discard her jeans and panties. She was already clawing at the button and zipper on his jeans, as he tried to get his wallet out of his back pocket. He almost dropped it when she wrapped her hand around his erection. Bending his head back, he closed his eyes and enjoyed the feel of her fingers as they danced over his sensitive flesh. Soon, though, he was close to losing it.

He batted her hands away and she giggled, the sound danced through him. He paused for the merest of moments and looked at her. He had said he loved her laugh before, but he didn't know just what that meant until this last assignment. He had thought of it during those long, cold, lonely nights. He had dreamed of her laugh for months. Hearing it in person loosened something in his chest and made his soul happy.

But he would enjoy it more later. Right now, he needed to be inside of her. He slipped the condom on. Entering her in one fast, hard thrust. They both groaned. He pulled her to the edge of the counter, thrusting over and over into her. He changed his position, deepening his strokes. He wanted to come right there and then, but he wanted her with him. He slipped his hand between the two of them and pressed her clit. That was all it took. Her inner muscles rippled over his cock, then her entire body convulsed against him. She screamed his name as she came. He thrust into her once more and gave in to his own release.

* * * *

Somehow they made it to her bedroom. Now, long moments later, with the sound of rain tapping against the windows, they cuddled on the bed, and Elena couldn't seem to stop touching him to assure herself JT really was back. She settled her head against JT's chest and sighed. Just having him there, safe and sound did the trick for her.

"What's wrong?" he asked.

She lifted her head and looked at him. Even in the dim light, she could still see the dark circles beneath his eyes. That, along with the weight loss, worried her. But now that he was back, she really didn't care about anything else.

"Nothing, just tired. And now I don't feel like going into work tomorrow."

"You could call in sick."

She smiled. "You know better. I get to fly tomorrow."

He rolled his eyes. Pilots in the military were well known for their single-mindedness when it came to the job. A day in the air was always better than a day on the ground. She definitely believed that. Of course, now that JT was back, it was hard to decide which would be better. A day in bed with him sounded divine.

"Besides, I'm taking Tuesday through Thursday off."

"Any reason?"

"Nope. I always have use-or-lose leave at the end of the year, so I learned to take a few days off here and there. Maybe it was just intuition."

"Maybe you wanted a few days to yourself when Brando left."

It was her turn to roll her eyes. "That was getting annoying."

"How long was he here?"

"Just a little over a week, but man, I was sick of him. Sick of all of them."

He frowned. "What's that mean?"

"Mom was worried about me. Seems I lost a little weight and have been preoccupied."

"I was going to mention that."

She groaned and fell back on the pillows. "Not you too. I am getting sick of people mentioning it." It was true she had lost weight, but it wasn't as if she was wasting away. "And you can't talk. I've dropped five pounds. You look like you've lost twenty."

He didn't say anything and she looked at him. Something passed over his expression that told her the mission had been bad. "Yeah, well, if I keep eating like tonight, I won't have a problem putting the weight back on."

"You can't talk about it?"

He shook his head. "Not yet."

"I have top secret clearance."

"And it's different because you're active duty. Truth is, I am not sure I will ever be able to talk about it much. Just being debriefed made me sick."

The weary tone of his voice hurt her. JT had always loved his job, so she hated that tone. "It was that bad?"

"Yeah. Worse than we'd thought. But, we got the guy in charge, so everything should be taken care of. It's just I can't understand why people have to go that way. Why sell out your fellow Marine to make a buck?"

JT was questioning more than what he had been though on the mission. He was thinking about his father.

An alcoholic and an abuser, his father was the epitome of horrible. They all knew the story and knew that until JT had stood up to his father, no one ever knew what was going on in his household. Harold Thomas had a chest full of medals, numerous high profile jobs, and he was the scum of the Earth. She knew that was one of the reasons JT had decided to get out of the military and work for

NCIS.

"Why does anyone? Some people have no morals. It's like they're missing the quotient to have empathy. They are in every walk of life."

But, JT was not one of them. She knew he worried about his background. He never really drank to excess, and he always kept his temper at a good level.

She set her head on his chest again, and he held her tighter. "Let's talk about normal things."

"Okay."

"Tell me what went on while I was gone?"

Elena smiled. She settled her head against his chest again. With the darkness of the night settled around them, she told him of the events from the last few months. She covered the romance between her best friend and her twin brother, the events that almost led to both of them being killed and their wedding.

"Lord, I feel like I've been gone for years."

She sighed. She was so happy to have him back; she couldn't hide how she felt. "It felt like you were gone for years."

He chuckled. The sound of it vibrated against her ear. "I can't believe Dante is married."

"I know. It's hard to deal with sometimes. But then, he's so damned happy, and he makes Madison happy. You should see them together. I don't think I have ever seen Madison smile so much. And Dante, forget about it. That man is head over heels in love with her. They are so freaking cute together."

He cleared his throat. "About this weight loss of yours…"

"Yeah?" she asked, but she rolled her eyes since he couldn't see her.

"I want you to be healthy."

She lifted her head and narrowed her eyes. "Right back at you mister."

He wasn't what most people would term skinny. He'd

lost weight but had gained muscle mass. He was now leaner, which accentuated his abs and his arms. But, she didn't like what his job did to him sometimes. She had seen it in her brother Anthony. He would lose weight, but he also had other outlets. Women and cussing were her oldest brother's outlets. JT was wound very tight.

"Don't worry. I said if you keep feeding me, I'll be fine."

Elena snorted. "Dream on. I am not going to cook for you all the time."

He pulled her over on top of him. "I could pay you for it."

"Is that a fact?" she asked, as little bursts of electric current slid through her blood.

He pursed his lips as if in deep thought. She had to bite her lip to keep from smiling. The man was adorable when he teased. She would have never in her life thought he was flirting. No man had ever made her forget the entire world by just looking at her. But he did. When he gave her that smile, an atomic bomb could go off outside of her apartment, and she probably wouldn't notice. "I have the impression that I'm pretty good in bed."

"Hmm." She said nothing else.

He frowned at her and she laughed.

His frown dissolved, and he stared at her much like he had when he'd shown up at her apartment.

"What?"

He shook his head. "I love hearing you laugh."

He had said it before in the same tone. Then he said nothing else. It was unnerving what he could do to her by just looking at her. Right now, her body was flushed with excitement and her pulse was hammering in her neck. It had nothing to do with laying naked in bed with him. She knew if they were across the room from each other and JT looked at her like that, she would feel it to the tips of her toes.

"Okay, stop that."

"Stop what?"

"Stop staring at me like that. I can't take it."

He raised one hand and cupped her jaw with it.

"I can't help it. For months now I've been remembering every curve, every edge to your body. There were times when I thought I could smell you in bed next to me. And every now and then, I was convinced I could hear your laugh. It kept me going, Elena. Just the thought of you here, safe, knowing that someday I would see you again. There were moments I was ready to lose it, and you are the one who brought me back from the edge."

She blinked as her vision wavered.

"Don't do that," he said.

She made a sound that could only be termed as rude. "Well, don't say things like that to me."

"No, I meant don't try to hide your emotions from me. I know that you think of yourself as one of the boys, but you don't have to be strong all the time with me. I don't think less of you when you show you're vulnerable."

She leaned down to kiss him. "Thank you."

"What for?"

"For wanting me just the way I am."

He chuckled as he rolled them over and reversed their positions. He was already hard against her sex.

"I would never try and tell you to change."

Then he started kissing his way down her body. He settled between her legs, placing a hand on each thigh and spread her legs further apart. She felt his breath the moment before his mouth touched her. He slipped his tongue inside of her. She could barely remember her name when he started to kiss his way back up her body.

He rested his weight on his hands then leaned down and kissed her. She could taste herself there; he pulled away to grab a condom. With quick movements, he had it on and was easing his way into her. She lifted her legs and wrapped them around his hips as he continued to thrust inside her. Soon, she was right there with him again, her body ready for another orgasm. He thrust into her so hard, the headboard slammed against the wall. Suddenly, in one blinding second she was falling, splintering apart into a million pieces as her release crashed over her. Just a moment later, JT shouted her name as he joined her in pleasure.

CHAPTER EIGHT

The next morning, Elena woke before her alarm went off. Carefully, she reached over and shut the alarm off before it could go off and wake JT. He needed his sleep, and they hadn't gotten much during the night, she thought with a smile.

It was hard to force herself away from JT. It was so toasty and warm laying beside him. For just a second or two, she thought about calling in sick. Of course, the thought didn't last that long. She had a duty and well, it was a flying day.

She slipped out of bed and headed to the shower. She had a few extra minutes this morning, but she still needed to be at work. Before she stepped into the bathroom, she looked back over her shoulder. She couldn't fight the smile that curved her lips. Seeing him there in her bed made her so damned happy. She wanted to say to hell with work and stay home, but she had to go. They had a training mission her new commander insisted on and besides, a Santini never shirked their duty.

After she shut the door as quietly as possible, she started the shower. The bathroom water took forever to heat up. It was one of the few things she hated about her apartment. It wasn't far from some good beaches, and it was close enough to work that she didn't have to worry about a long commute.

As she waited for the water to heat up, she thought about what JT had said the night before. It sounded as if he was planning on sticking around. She had hoped for that, but she really didn't know how he would act when he returned. Guys often said things they regretted later. Hell, not just guys. Both sexes did things like that. It was easy enough to see every day in the military. She didn't think that every person who did it, did it on purpose. The kind of jobs they had, life was always precious. Knowing you had someone waiting on you when you returned made it easier to get through the mission. It wasn't the right thing to do, but when faced with a dangerous assignment, people didn't always make the best decisions.

For Elena, she might not always have a man at home, but she had an overbearing family she adored. She knew there were a lot of people like JT. Of course, her family was his family, and they would have to deal with that entanglement later. Right now, she just wanted him to herself. Elena knew it was important that they had this time alone to get to know each other.

She smiled. They knew each other in different ways, but now they needed to explore what was going on between them. She looked forward to getting to know every one of his irritating qualities.

The room started to fill up with steam, and she knew she needed to stop daydreaming about things. She stepped into the shower with a new mission. The sooner she got her work done, the sooner she had three days to spend alone with JT.

* * * *

JT rolled over and reached for Elena. Instead, he found her pillow and an empty bed. He frowned and slowly opened his eyes. He blinked. It was still pitch black in the room. He looked at the clock she had on the bedside table and noticed it was near four in the morning.

Damn, it was too early for him. Where was Elena?

He heard the shower going. He wanted to join her. The memories of that Saturday morning shower together had haunted his dreams and left him yearning for another experience like that for months. He couldn't join her. He'd make her late. He knew she had work, and he hated that she was going to be gone today. It was selfish, but he wanted her all to himself at least for a few days. Or weeks.

He rolled over onto his back and stared at the ceiling. He knew she had a job. He also had to check in with his boss. They had a few things to discuss. He also had to call Anthony. For the last few years, Anthony had been the one person he always called once he was cleared. Now, he hadn't thought about it until that precise moment. JT didn't even have to think about it. He knew it was because someone else was more important now.

He grabbed another pillow, stacking them so he could be more comfortable. He knew his life had changed that Friday night when Elena had asked for a ride home. He had known it the moment he'd kissed her. It was as if something had clicked in his soul. Even he hadn't felt that with his ex-fiancé.

Bethany had been a wonderful woman and, for a brief moment, he had thought she was the one for him. He sighed. That was a lie. He *wanted* her to be the one for him. She was stable and easy. And now, he realized how sad those were the two things he remembered most. She didn't fight, not really, at least toward the end. He'd thought he could make it work, but both of them decided that it wasn't going to. He heard she married a lawyer last year and was already expecting her first child.

That thought made him think of what Elena would look like pregnant. Funny, he never thought of Bethany that way while they were engaged. He never looked beyond what marriage was going to mean. A lifetime together, building a family, a happy life. It had all been about having a woman who didn't really bother him. Damn, he was an asshole.

With a sigh, he stifled the need to tell Elena exactly how he felt. He couldn't say anything just yet. She would freak out if he did. Elena might talk a good game, but he didn't know exactly what she wanted out of the relationship. She was younger than he was, by a few years, and she was just getting her career off the ground. Not telling her family was one thing, but he wasn't going to let that go for long. Sooner or later, Dante was going to open his big mouth and tell the others.

He noticed the light went out in the bathroom and the door opened. She was standing there wearing only a towel. She'd brushed her damp hair away from her face, and now that his eyes had adjusted to the light, he could see her. He loved her this way, all natural with no makeup.

Lust coiled tight in his stomach, as heat shifted through his veins. He couldn't help it. Just looking at her like that had him ready to pull her back in bed. JT had a feeling it was always going to be like this—probably until the day he died.

"I'm sorry, I was trying to be quiet," she said.

"No problem and you didn't wake me. Woke up on my own."

She nodded and headed to her closet. She opened the double doors, then stepped inside, shutting the door slightly. A shaft of light illuminated the room, but not directly in his eyes.

"Do you have anything planned today?" she asked.

"I have to head up to the office to talk to the boss. Afterwards, I have to go pick up my mail."

"Sounds good."

She stepped back out wearing a pair of boy short panties and a sports bra. She was holding her flight suit in one hand and her boots in another. She dropped the boots beside the bed, then stepped into her uniform. As she slipped her arms into the sleeves, then yanked it up over her shoulders, a delicious thrill layered over the simmering lust. He drew in a breath then released it quietly. Damn, watching her dress in her uniform was definitely a turn on.

"I shouldn't be late since we are doing the runs this morning. I have a few reports to check on, but it's just tying up some things before my days off."

Damn, she was freaking sexy and she was his. It was something to know the woman beneath that uniform. It was like a special little secret they shared with just each other.

She smiled at him. "What?"

He shrugged. "It's sexy to watch you get ready for work. That uniform is kind of hot."

She laughed and joined him on the bed. "Yeah? Being a pilot does get me some attention. But, I bet you'll enjoy it more when it comes off."

She gave him a kiss, then slipped out of bed. Picking up her boots, she said, "I'll leave an extra key on the counter in the kitchen. Make yourself at home."

She walked out of the room and left him to his thoughts. He heard her leaving a few minutes later.

He continued to stare at the ceiling. Lord, the woman didn't know what she was doing to him. There was no doubt she wouldn't have taken a chance on him if she wasn't serious, but work needed to be sorted out. He wanted to be here, be part of her life, but there were a few things he had to get set into motion before that would happen.

Deciding it was better to get up and get on with his day, he forced himself out of bed and into the bathroom.

* * * *

Elena was almost out of the door when her commanding officer caught her.

"Captain Santini," Colonel Vent yelled out.

She was so close to getting out of there that she wanted to scream. Still, the day had been good, and the training had been challenging. She liked that and thrived on it. It was one of the aspects she really liked about Vent. He might be an ass, but he challenged them and that made her happy. It made her a better Marine.

So, just as all Santinis did, she gritted her teeth. She might not like him, but she respected him.

She turned to face him. "Yes, sir?"

"I understand you took the next few days off."

She nodded. "You approved it a couple weeks ago."

"Is there a particular reason?"

She wondered just how many times he had questioned the men she flew with. "No. I wanted a few days off, and I always have use-or-lose time at the end of the year."

He nodded. "Make sure you make yourself available if need be."

She blinked. "Is there something I don't know about?"

"No. I had an issue with Lt. Marks. He didn't have his cell nearby, and we couldn't get a hold of him."

Which made sense. This was his first assignment. "Yes, sir. I am actually just staying in town, so no worries."

"You're dismissed."

He turned and walked away. Elena caught herself before she gritted her teeth. At this rate, she would have to be fitted with dentures by the end of the year. She didn't always make friends with her commanders, but they rarely took a dislike to her like this one. He was always on her case about things. Since he'd arrived six months ago, he had made more than one comment about her taking time off. It was hard not to take some leave while her parents and the rest of the Santinis had descended on Southern California for Dante's wedding. And she was the freaking maid of honor. She had things to do.

She brushed those thoughts away. She had a man to go see. Stepping out into the parking lot, something stirred on the back of her neck as if someone were watching her. She looked behind her, but noticed only a few folks in the parking lot. None of them were looking at her. Shrugging it off, she continued walking to her car, but she felt it again. Instead of looking around, she ignored it. She hadn't had much sleep, and it had been a tough training mission. Add in her feelings towards the new commander, and it added up to weird feelings.

She slipped into her car and decided that the next few days would cure her of any issues. She was pretty sure JT would dispel any worries she had. With a smile, she strapped on her seatbelt and started the engine. She definitely had more than a few things they could do to forget worries for at least a few days.

CHAPTER NINE

Three wonderful days later, Elena smiled at herself in the mirror as she pulled her hair up into a ponytail. It had been the most wonderful seventy-two hours of her life. She was even including the first time she got in a cockpit to fly. Spending time with JT alone had been amazing. She knew him so well, but Elena felt as if she had ripped another layer of complexity away and knew him even better. Granted, the sex had been mind-blowing, but there was more to it than that. Even in the short time she had with him, she had found out so much more about him.

She'd decided to go ahead and take the entire rest of the week off. After a call to her commander, she had gotten one more day added to her leave. She had so much leave and time was running out to use it. With an inspection this fall, she knew they would have a lot of work ahead of them. At least now, she wouldn't just have the leave dissolve. And well, JT was definitely worth a little leave.

They were finally leaving the apartment; although, she would have been perfectly happy to stay there until Monday morning. JT said they needed sun and since was a beautiful day, she suggested the beach

She grabbed her cover up and tugged it over her head as she walked into her bedroom. Since she'd gotten home Monday night, they had spent every moment together. They hadn't even left for food. They had just eaten what she had, then started to order out. And, they always seemed to find themselves in bed. Not just for sex. They ate in there too. And talked. They did so much talking. Not anything serious, just little things like regular couples did.

But she could almost feel JT's need to set things right with her family. It irritated her on one level. She was a grown woman, and the United States Marine Corps trusted her with millions of dollars of hardware every day she went up in the air. So, the fact that he thought they needed to tell her family about her relationship didn't make sense to her. On that level.

On another level, the one that encased her heart and drew her even closer to him, she admired it. He respected her and her family. It was the only reason he wanted to clear the air. Plus, it also spoke of his commitment to their relationship.

That word made her pause for a second. *Relationship.* She realized she was standing there grinning at herself in her dresser mirror, and she looked like a fool. But she didn't care. She was in a relationship with Jethro Thomas, the man she had been in love with for most of her adult life.

So, she needed to be careful. They needed time to get to know each other better without the scrutiny of her family. If things went bad, she knew they would blame JT, and she didn't want that. She knew they considered him family, and she couldn't bear it if something ruined that.

She shook those worries away. She made sure she had her sunglasses in her bag, as she practically skipped out into the living room. It had been a long time since she'd been to the beach and even though there would still be a lot of tourists, she was okay with that.

JT smiled at her. "I thought you said you didn't want to leave. You look pretty happy to me about it."

"Truthfully, I am pretty happy about the beach. And although it will make me sound like a goofball, I'm just happy to be going with you."

His eyes warmed and his smile widened as he walked toward her. "Is that so?"

He slipped his arm around her waist and pulled her against him. "Maybe we should forget going to the beach."

He finished the sentence the moment before he brushed his mouth against hers. He didn't close his eyes. By the time he pulled back, her body was humming with need and excitement, and she couldn't remember why they thought it was a good idea going out.

"Let's stay here," she said, pulling him back to her mouth. She kissed him as if her life depended on it. By the time he pulled back, they were both breathing heavily.

He shook his head. "No. We're going. We need some vitamin D, and maybe we should make sure this isn't just about sex."

She wanted to tell him it wasn't. She knew without a doubt she loved him. But, guys freaked out about things like that.

"Plus, I'm not sure I can keep up with you. I am getting a little too old for this."

She let one eyebrow rise as she slipped on her flip-flops. "Is that so? Do you mean you used to make love more than four or five times a day when you were younger?"

He chuckled. "What can I say? You make me feel young."

She smiled. "Well, that's good."

She walked past him and he shook his head. "I should have known you were going to be trouble."

"Just remember that when I irritate you."

* * * *

JT had just settled on his towel as Elena pulled off her cover up. It had been hard to force himself out of that apartment, especially since she didn't want to go, but now he was going to have to see her like this. Damn, the woman was practically naked.

Okay, it wasn't any worse than most of the woman on the beach, but she was wearing a bright blue bikini that barely covered all the important parts.

She handed him some sunscreen lotion. "Do me."

He studied her for a second. Her sunglasses hid her eyes, but her smile told him she was daring him to say something. The woman had a warped sense of humor. He could tell from her smile, she was daring him to say something. He said nothing and waited for her to sit down on her towel.

"It's not as crowded as I thought it would be," she said as he poured the lotion in his hand and rubbed it on her back.

"Middle of the week."

"But it's summer. I thought there would be more tourists."

He said nothing to that. He couldn't. It was hard touching her like this on a public beach and not being able to do more. Inwardly, he scoffed. He had said he was worried it was all about sex. He knew for himself, that wasn't true.

JT wanted forever. The fact that he still wasn't freaking out about that had him itching to call her father. But they hadn't really dated, not for long, and she had been right. They needed time together before they had family intruding. There was one thing the Santini family was good at and that was intruding. Secondly, he needed to talk to Anthony. His friend needed to know up front that he had fallen in love with his sister.

"So, I guess we proved this isn't about sex."

He sighed and leaned forward so he could whisper in her ear. "It is taking all my control not to pull you down on the towel and ravish you."

She laughed. "Sure."

"Seriously."

She turned and looked at him. The smile she wore did little to cool his need for her. In fact, that sassy grin made her even more attractive. He loved confident women, and Elena had confidence in spades.

"I believe you, but that doesn't matter," she said.

"It doesn't matter?"

She shook her head. "Nope. My parents are still like that. And so embarrassing at times."

"What do you mean?"

She sighed and settled on her towel. "At Dante and Madison's wedding reception, my parents couldn't keep their hands off each other. It was embarrassing that they were getting more comments than even the newlyweds. They danced the Tango, and there was little doubt that Dante wasn't the only Santini getting lucky that night."

"I think it's nice." And it was. The fact that her parents had been married for so long and still adored each other was comforting. He'd wanted that all his life. Some kind of woman who could stand up to him as much as she attracted him.

Until now, he just never thought it would be Elena. But he knew without a doubt, he would be just like her father—like all the Santini men for that matter.

"Well, it would be okay if they weren't my parents. Jesus, they have six kids. You would think by now they would know how to behave."

"They did have six children. There's a reason."

She made a face. "I don't want to think about it."

JT smiled and settled back on his towel. With a sigh, he enjoyed the feel of the sun on his skin, and the fact that he was spending time with the woman beside him.

Life couldn't get better than this.

* * * *

By the time they got home that afternoon, Elena was more than happy to just pick up a pizza and then eat it in bed. JT had different ideas. He made her go shopping with him. Apparently, big, bad NCIS agent liked to have fresh fruit, and he decided to make her dinner.

After both of them showered, she watched him make her dinner. It was a novel thing. Not that a man was cooking, but that a man was cooking for her. Other than family, she didn't know any man who had offered to do that for her.

"Now, where did you learn to cook?" she asked as she took a long sip of her wine.

He smiled but didn't look up. "Your brother taught me this particular recipe."

He spread the pizza sauce on top of the naan bread, then grabbed the bag of cheese. He sprinkled a generous amount on both of the pizzas and looked at her.

"You wanted mushrooms, onions, and pepperoni?"

She nodded. He had even sautéed the mushrooms just the way she liked them. Lifting her foot up on the chair, she settled back.

"You know, a girl could get used to this. It would be much more interesting if you would have just worn the apron and nothing else like I suggested."

He opened the oven and put the pizzas in. After he shut the door, he smiled at her. "We would have never eaten. And while the apron does protect me a bit, I'm not too keen on having my important bits around a hot stove."

She laughed, enjoying him and stood up. She gave him a long, hot, wet kiss.

"Let's just go to bed," she said.

He groaned. "No. We need to sit here and eat."

She pouted.

"Okay, we'll take it to bed and eat it there."

"Aww, look there, a compromise."

She gave him another fast kiss, then grabbed a couple of plates down from the cupboard. Now, she just had to get them through dinner as fast as possible, so she could get her hands on the man again.

* * * *

Terror clogged his throat, as he stood there in the kitchen where he'd had more than one dinner.

"You bastard."

It was his father's favorite name for him. JT used to take it, but now, he was eighteen and he refused. He was leaving, and he wasn't ever coming back.

"You think I am going to let you walk out that door?"

"I'm eighteen now. I can do whatever the hell I want."

"The fuck you can," his father said, coming at him with the two by four he'd been holding when he walked into the kitchen. His father raised it up and swung it towards his head.

Elena woke up the moment she heard JT yell out. She sat up, her heartbeat a tattoo against her chest as she tried to figure out what the hell was going on and where she was. Drawing in huge gulps of air, she felt someone thrashing against her.

JT.

She looked down at him. His face was twisted in pain, his head back as if someone was hurting him. He was murmuring something she couldn't understand, but she knew it was something that was scaring the living hell out of him.

"JT, wake up."

He shook his head, too lost to the pain that was going on his head. She shook him and he lashed out. He barely missed punching her jaw. She stumbled back just out of reach. He blinked and sat up.

"What?" he asked, his gaze still unfocused. He looked like he had one foot in reality and one foot back in the dream.

"You were having a bad dream."

He shook his head as if trying to clear it. He looked up

at her. Even in the dark light, she saw his face pale.

"I almost hit you."

She heard the tone, the self-loathing. His father was on his mind again. Something about this mission had brought it up for him.

"You were having a nightmare, and I should have known better. Dante would have them sometimes and lash out if anyone tried to wake him up."

"I'm sorry."

She scooted closer and cupped his face. "You were having a bad dream. When I woke you up, you struck out. A lot of people do it. Do you remember what you were dreaming about?"

He nodded, but she knew he didn't want to talk about it.

"I take it you would rather not talk."

"It was the last time I saw my father."

When his father had beaten him for standing up to him. He'd ended up in the hospital.

"Oh, Jethro."

"Don't pity me."

She shook her head. "Never. I would never pity a man who came from that situation and made a life for himself. I admire you and I hurt for you, but I don't pity you."

She didn't know what else to say. So she did the one thing she knew he needed. Leaning forward, she kissed him lightly, then deepened it. He hesitated at first, then groaned. He slipped his arms around her waist and pulled her on top of him. He rolled them over so that their positions were reversed.

Without hesitation, she gave herself to him. Their lovemaking was fevered and fast…and perfect. He needed this from her, and she needed to give it to him. Moments later, as they both crested over the edge into pleasure, she felt as if she had been stripped bare.

CHAPTER TEN

Monday morning, JT made his way into the office. When he stopped by last week, his boss had been in a meeting. JT had another week of leave left, but he really wanted to set things straight with his boss, Vic Glover. He didn't want to talk about forever with Elena if he didn't have everything set in motion.

JT stepped off the elevator and into the cubicle-laden room he'd spent too much time in. The buzz of work filled the air as he walked down the hallway to his division. He nodded to a few people but didn't stop to chat. He had made a decision and he had to talk to Vic. He found him at his desk. Since his divorce a couple of years earlier, Vic spent most of his time at the office.

Vic saw him when he was halfway across the room. As he walked into the office, he realized that the last few years had been hard on Vic. He was only a few years older than JT, but Vic looked as if he had ten years on JT. An inch or two taller than JT's six-three frame, he kept his hair military short. The graying at the temples spoke of the stress he had been through. Running an investigative team with NCIS wasn't easy on anyone.

He stood as JT approached the desk. The frown wasn't anything new. The man was never happy, but this seemed to be directed at JT.

"What are you doing in today? Gregory isn't going to let you come back to work so quickly."

JT shook his head. He knew the head honcho wasn't

going to be happy if he thought JT was in there trying to work. Undercover assignments took a lot out of a person. Taking time to bring yourself back into your own life was important. It was also mandatory.

"No, I wanted to talk to you about my future."

"Aw, shit." Vic sighed. "I had a feeling."

"You did?"

"Before you left, there was something off about you. I wasn't sure what it was, but I knew this might be the last one. I hate for you to let that investigation get to you. You're too good of an investigator."

JT shook his head. Things had been bad on the UA this time. But, it wasn't as if he hadn't gone through some crap before.

"It wasn't the assignment. I have other things I want to do."

His face fell further. It was comical. "Damn. You found a woman."

"Yeah."

"I guess I can't warn you the job takes a toll."

He shook his head. Vic's marriage hadn't been great, but his workaholic ways didn't help the matter. The divorce two years ago had made him even worse.

"She's a woman who understands duty."

"Is that a fact? They all say that." Skepticism dripped from every word.

JT chuckled. "No, believe me, the family is born and bred military."

"Damn. Okay. Is there any way I can convince you to stay? "

He felt his eyes widen. "Good God, I'm not resigning. I just don't want a UA."

Vic's frown eased into something close to a smile. Well, as close as Vic got to a smile. "Oh. I can handle that. I was going to suggest you take a break anyway, but I wasn't sure how you would handle it."

He shrugged. "I probably would have fought it before

her, but then, I didn't have anything to come home to."

His boss settled his hands on his hips and shook his head. "Damn, I am going to have to meet the woman who makes you speak like that. Who would have thought it?"

"I'm sure you'll meet her soon."

Truth was, Vic knew her. He'd met Elena once or twice when Anthony had been assigned to the office. That was the one thing he knew he would have to face soon. His best friend was never going to accept this situation, but he had to be the one to tell him up front.

"I did want to talk to you," Vic said, looking around and motioning with his head to come back to his cubicle.

"What about?" JT asked, wondering at the strange behavior.

"We think there is something more on the case."

That stopped his brain from functioning for a second or two.

"No. Smith was the guy. He controlled everything."

The last few months had been about drug running and illegal gun sales. Several assholes had decided to sell military weapons to get money to buy drugs. Once they had them, they'd started to sell them around the base and the areas around the base. It had been one of the worst cases he'd worked on in his career. The lack of empathy those bastards had for other people, including their fellow military members, had almost sent him over the edge. More than once a military member who had nothing to do with the operation had been affected. And, since many of the drugs had been sold on and around military bases, it indirectly affected them also.

And the bastards just didn't care.

"He's talking to the justice department. We aren't sure about what, but rumor is that he is trying to get a deal."

"Fuck." That meant he had something. The Justice Department wouldn't go near him if he didn't have evidence of someone else involved.

"Exactly."

If Smith was getting a deal, it meant he would do little to no time. It also meant they missed someone. The captain had been charged with a multitude of crimes. He'd controlled the entire operation out of his office on base. JT had never met a person who had such low morals, and that was saying a lot considering his father. Worse, Smith had always been the epitome of the perfect Marine officer. He appeared to be the perfect family man. But, beneath the impeccable façade lay the dirtiest of scum. JT had thought the man would sell his children to get ahead.

"I just wanted to give you a heads up just in case."

JT nodded.

"Give me a call on my cell if anything pops."

As JT headed back out to his truck, his mind wasn't on the woman who had consumed most of his thoughts lately. He was mentally rerunning the case, trying to think of anything he might have missed. One thing was for sure; he wasn't going back under. All the investigating would have to be done on this side of the work. He had something more important to attend to.

With that thought, he hurried to his truck and decided to stop by his house to pick up his mail. Then, he would head off to Elena's.

* * * *

After filling up at the gas station on base, Elena started on her way home. For Monday, it had been an easy day. She knew JT had run into work for a bit, and it was good to have some time apart. She had never been a woman who looked for her identity in a man. It wasn't that she didn't want one in her life, but she would rather he stand beside her and make her stronger. With her career field of flying Raptors, she was consumed with work a lot of the time. Everyone in the military who had dealt with a pilot knew that a pilot's focus was on his or her job. It was just the way it had to be. One little mistake could cost you your life.

Concentrating had been a problem today. Of course, she'd been thinking about JT all day long. It had been irritating to be called out by people for not paying attention. Now if she had a chance to fly today, it would have been okay. It was the one thing in the world that had kept her sane while JT had been gone.

From the time she was five, she had wanted to be a pilot. Her mother had told her that she had talked about it nonstop after seeing the Air Force Thunderbirds, but she really didn't want to go Air Force. It wasn't until she was a freshman in high school that she decided she wanted to do it for the Marines. She was thrilled to be living in a time when women had a chance, no matter how slight, to try for flight.

Things in her life seemed to be falling into place. Now, if she could just let things be with JT. She knew she was pushy. It was hard not to be in her family. Growing up with three older brothers and a twin hadn't been easy on her. Hell, when Nando appeared on the scene, he had even tried to tell her what to do. His first word was *no* and it was directed at her. All of them had made sure that she grew up with a chip on her shoulder and an attitude to be able to carry it. It was one of the reasons she hadn't wanted to let the family know about their relationship. They needed time to figure out where they stood. And hopefully, she could keep herself from being too pushy. As she turned down the two-lane highway that led to her apartment, Elena knew she needed to start thinking about a house. Granted, she rarely had anything bigger than what she had now. Her work took a lot of her time, and she didn't need a lot of space. Now that JT was in the picture, she felt as if she needed to give him his own area. Men liked that; she knew that from experience.

Glancing up in her rearview mirror, she noticed a car approaching at a rapid pace. She frowned. It wasn't that deserted on the road, but she didn't like the way the guy was coming up on her. There was no shoulder for her to pull over on.

The car raced forward then pulled back. Over and over he did it. She gripped the wheel and just continued to drive. It might just be an asshole who wanted her to go faster, but she was already five miles an hour over the speed limit.

Quickly, he raced forward and pulled up alongside of her. It was a no passing zone, and she didn't want to have an accident, so she eased off the gas, thinking she would let him pass. He kept pace, slowing down with her. Panic started to beat in her blood, as the car inched closer beside her. There was no one nearby. She glanced over and realized the windows were tinted so dark, she would never be able to see who it was. She didn't even know if it was a man or not.

Elena looked up in her mirror. There was no one behind her. She slammed on her breaks, just as the car beside her suddenly veered to the right. He barely clipped the front fender of her car. She watched as the car sped off down the road. Her hands were shaking as she drew in a few breaths.

Her head was spinning and no small wonder. She might be an adrenaline junkie when it came to flying, but she didn't mess around on the road. When she got herself pulled together, she decided to head home. She had more important things to worry about than some jackass with a death wish.

CHAPTER ELEVEN

Elena splashed some water on her face. Her hands were still shaking as she tried to get over the near encounter. Her heart wasn't beating out of control and she wasn't really scared anymore. She was pissed. Just because some ass wanted to get around her, he had almost killed her.

There was one thing she couldn't accept, and that was treating life so frivolously. Santinis understood how precious it was, especially after almost losing Carlos when he was shot on his last deployment. Playing around on a highway was unacceptable. She had been so shaken up that she had forgotten to get the car tag. And without it, there really wasn't much she could do. She would call and file a report, but past that, she knew nothing would come of it.

Wiping off her face, she pushed away the rest of her worries. She'd wait until JT got home and she would talk to him about it. He'd probably tell her she should call the police, if only to report reckless driving.

She hung up the towel and was contemplating dinner when her cell phone rang. She wanted to ignore it, knowing that JT should be there soon, but a certain dark knight's heavy breathing told her it was her mother.

"Hey, Mama," she said, thankful her voice didn't shake.

"Elena, do you still have that horrible ringtone?"

"No," she said, easily lying to her mother.

"Hmm, I have a feeling you're not telling me the truth." But apparently she wasn't going to push it. "How are you doing?"

"I'm fine. Although, I had a long boring day."

Her mother laughed. "So, no flying?"

Her mother knew her too well. It was one of the reasons she had been very careful the last couple of times they'd talked on the phone. She knew after the wedding, her mother had been really worried. Marcella Santini knew that if her daughter wasn't eating, there was something wrong. And, just like all the other mothers in the Santini family, she felt it was her right to pry.

"No. But I should get to fly tomorrow, so that's all good. Now why don't you tell me why you are calling?"

"I just wanted to hear your voice."

She sighed and decided her mother would keep dancing around the subject. "Please, quit checking up on me."

"What do you mean?"

She sighed. "You aren't even being subtle. Carlos has called three times this month. I don't think I've ever talked to him so much—even when we lived in the same house. Brando was the worst houseguest. If I didn't take him out, he expected me to cook for him. And we both know that idiot can cook better than I can. He whined and complained the entire time he was here. There is a good chance if he had stayed one more day, I might have killed him. Or, gotten him drunk and shaved off one eyebrow while he was sleeping."

Her mother didn't say anything for a moment. That meant she was probably trying to decide whether to keep lying or come clean.

"I've been worried about you."

Her heart squeezed tight. As the only females in the family, they had always been close. They saw themselves as the embattled females and, thanks to her mother, Elena knew just how to push back when it came to all men, her brothers included. She was still one of her closest confidants, but she couldn't tell her exactly why she was doing well, but she wanted to reassure her.

"I know you have, but things are going better."

"Good. I hear it in your voice."

"You do?" she asked, still always mystified by her mother's ability to ferret out that her children were having problems.

"Yes. At the wedding, you were unhappy."

She frowned, hoping that other people didn't think she was upset about Madison and Dante marrying. Nothing made her happier than seeing them get married.

"I was not. I was so happy for Madison and Dante."

"Oh, I know you were happy for them, and you hid it well." She sighed again. "No one else could tell, but I am your mother. I know when you are hurt."

"I wasn't hurt."

Another pause. "Lonely then. Missing someone."

She sighed. "Yes."

"But that seems to be solved now."

The door opened and JT came in. He was smiling until he saw her face. It slowly transformed into a concerned frown. He looked so cute like that. Granted, she was pretty sure, he looked cute doing anything, but when he was concerned about her, he was irresistible.

"Elena?" her mother asked, concern in her voice.

Slowly, her lips curved. "Oh, yeah for sure."

"Who is it?" JT whispered.

"It's Mom."

"You have company," her mother said.

Well, she couldn't hide it and, truthfully, there wasn't anything weird about JT being at her apartment. He'd been part of their family for so long that it was actually expected.

"JT is here."

A pause. "Oh. Let me talk to him. He didn't call me when he returned."

She smiled, knowing that JT was going to get yelled at.

"Mom wants to talk to you," she said handing him the phone.

He took it with a frown on his lips. Elena just grinned at him.

"Hey, Mrs. S, how is everything going with you?"

Elena stepped closer and slid her arms around his waist. God, it always felt as if she had been starving for affection when she went longer than an hour or two without some kind of contact. She needed this, the warmth of his body and the vibration of his chest as he talked on the phone. She just needed him.

"I've been kind of busy."

She smiled as she kissed his throat. Her mother was definitely giving him hell. Elena could hear the rapid-fire questions thrown at him by her mother and figured he deserved it. They all knew they needed to call when they returned. Hell, even when she took a trip, she had to call when she arrived. Marcella Santini didn't like missing her children.

"Yes, yes, I know you worry."

Elena dragged her teeth over his flesh, and he shuddered.

"No. I don't want you to worry about me anymore. I promise to call when I return from assignments from now on."

More talking on the other end. Her mother was still asking him all kinds of questions. Elena lifted her head to kiss him along his jawline.

"No. No, we're just going out to eat," he said, his voice deepening.

Elena pressed against him and had to fight a moan. He was already hard beneath his jeans. She had always had a healthy sex drive, but JT had her behaving as if she were a sex addict. She couldn't keep her hands off him if he was in the room.

"Yeah, yeah, I promise. Did you want to talk to

Elena?" JT asked, as he closed his eyes.

Elena slipped her fingers beneath the waistband of his jeans, and he sucked in a breath. Her fingers brushed the tip of his erection. She glanced up and found him glaring at her.

"Okay, I'll talk to you later."

He clicked her phone off. The look he gave her told her she was in trouble. Oh, damn. He was so sweet when he was mad like this. And delicious.

She removed her hand from his pants and took a step back from him.

"You are in so much trouble."

Two seconds ticked by, then she screamed and ran. He caught up to her easily, and they fell on the bed together. Worries about work and family dissolved as they came together…beneath the setting California sun.

* * * *

Marcella stared out the window looking at the desert landscape, trying to come to terms with what she just heard in her daughter's voice. She blinked back the tears. Her baby girl was in love, and with a man Marcella respected. When she had heard JT, she knew there was more than just going to dinner. The two of them might think they were fooling her, but they weren't.

There had been a lot of close calls in the last few years, but she had always known Elena was waiting for someone. While her daughter had been content with some of her boyfriends, none of them had ever made Elena sound the way she did just now. There was so much happiness in her voice, Marcella could feel it over the phone.

Memories of the last couple of decades danced through her mind. She had known her daughter had a crush on JT for a long time, but somewhere, the stupid man had finally realized Elena was now a woman. And he was in love. He might not realize it, but Marcella knew that Jethro would never have slept with Elena if he wasn't in love with her.

Since she hadn't heard from any of her sons about this, she assumed they didn't know. Well, except Dante. Twins had a different view of sibling relations. As a mother of two sets, she knew that was true. They shared confidences, even with Dante and Elena being different sexes.

Elena and Jethro. Oh, they were going to be a wonderful couple, if they didn't screw it up. Of course, Jethro was a man, so there was a good chance he would. She had raised Elena to think for herself, so Marcella was certain that she would make sure JT fixed whatever he messed up.

"Hey," Tony said as he stepped into her home office.

Her heart did a little dance when she saw him. It had been that way for over thirty-five years, and she knew it would be the same until the day she died. He had a few more lines around his eyes, and his hair was half gray, but he was still the sweet man who had made her believe in love again.

"Is there something wrong?" he asked.

She shook her head. "I think we need to make a trip soon. Check up on Dante and Elena."

"We were just up there."

"I know, but I think it's important to pop up there. Truthfully, we both know we're lucky to have both of them so close at the same time.

He cocked his head to the side. "Something you want to tell me about?"

"No."

He smiled and pulled her into his arms. "I do have my ways of finding out what you've got going on up in that head of yours."

She shook her head. "I think you are too sure of yourself."

"Is that a fact?" he asked wiggling his eyebrows. With ease, he bent down and picked her up into his arms.

She laughed. "Put me down."

"I will when I find a flat surface."

She laughed as he carried her out of the room. The worries about her daughter could wait for now.

CHAPTER TWELVE

Elena poured the water for the coffee into her coffee maker when a knock sounded at the door. She frowned. It was more than a little odd that someone would come this early on a Saturday. Most of her friends were single and slept in on Saturdays. They also knew not to show up unannounced. Her first instinct was to ignore it. She wasn't in the mood to deal with anyone other than JT today. But the knocking was persistent.

With a sigh, she walked to the door and looked through the peephole. Her brother Anthony was standing there. Damn, she should have gone with her first instinct.

"Hurry up, Elena, I am tired as hell," Anthony said through the door.

"Anthony, what are you doing here?"

"I'll tell you when you finally open the damned door."

She opened the door. Her brother smiled. "You make a guy think his sister doesn't want to see him."

Before she could react, he stepped over the threshold and dumped a duffle on the floor beside the door, stepped in and gave her a big hug, lifting her up off her feet like he'd done for as long as she could remember.

He set her back down and shut the door.

"Why didn't you call?" she asked, glancing to make sure that JT hadn't come out.

He shrugged in that annoying way he had. Anthony worked on his own schedule and expected everyone to fall into line. Her mother said it had to do with him being the first of six siblings. Elena thought it was because he was stubborn as a mule. A mule with horrible, horrible timing.

"I was planning on bunking at JT's, but he isn't answering his phone. I went by his place this morning, and he wasn't there."

Something behind her caught his attention, and his smile faded, and she didn't need to turn around to know that JT had just walked out of her bedroom.

"What the fuck is going on here?" Anthony said, his voice shimmering with confusion and anger.

"None of your damned business," she said.

He hadn't taken his gaze away from JT. She glanced behind her and inwardly winced. JT was wearing a pair of boxers and nothing else.

"I wasn't asking you." Every word was said from behind clenched teeth.

"I can explain," JT said.

Anthony didn't give him a chance.

"You bastard," Anthony roared as he charged past Elena to tackle JT. He ignored her attempt to stop him as he flew past her. Both he and JT went crashing to the floor. As they rolled around on the carpet, they traded punches. The sickening sound of knuckles against flesh filled the apartment. Anthony continued to call his best friend the worst of names.

"Both of you stop it!"

They ignored her and rolled over and bumped her coffee table. A glass of water went flying onto the floor. Thankfully, it didn't break. They paid no attention whatsoever. Growing up in a boy-filled household told her just what she needed to do. She'd had enough of their crap, and this was going to stop now. She went to the kitchen and grabbed the spray bottle she used to water her plants. She hurried back and started to spray the idiots with water.

JT had pinned Anthony to the floor, but it only took a little water for him to stop fighting. Anthony, never one to miss a chance to win, took the opening and gave JT a good, hard right hook.

"Anthony, stop it." He was still ignoring her, so she used the only thing she had in her arsenal that would scare him. "I'll call Mama."

That had him pausing. His nose was bleeding and more than likely broken, but it was hard to tell. Anthony had broken his nose twice before—that she knew of.

She turned to look at JT. His lip was bleeding, and she was pretty sure he would end up with some bruises on his ribs.

She motioned with her head. "Come on, let's get you cleaned up."

"Hey," Anthony said. It sounded nasally. Yep, a broken nose. Served the big idiot right.

She looked him. "You started it. Go over to the sink to clean up, and don't bleed on my carpet."

She led JT back to her bathroom. "I'm sorry."

"I knew it would happen," he said, weariness in his voice. She didn't like the way that sounded one bit.

She shook her head and turned on the water before grabbing a washcloth. She wet it and dabbed at his lip. He winced.

"Sorry about that too. And it's stupid."

He studied her for a long moment as she continued to clean his lip. When she turned to rinse off the washcloth, he said, "You don't understand much about older brothers."

"I don't. They all have their own rules and regs for themselves, and a separate set for me. Even Nando gets their rules and he's a baby."

He sighed. "I want to stay, but I think your brother and you need to talk."

"I think you're right."

He kissed her nose then winced again.

"I need to go back to my apartment anyway, check my mail."

She nodded, but she didn't like it. For some reason, she felt abandoned. No, that wasn't it. She didn't want to be separated from him. It wasn't like her at all. She had never been the clingy type. And she knew he was right. She did need to talk to Anthony. For his part, Anthony needed to be hit upside the head a few times.

"Hey," JT said grabbing her chin. "I'll be back in a couple of hours."

She nodded again and watched as he grabbed a pair of jeans and stepped into them. He grabbed his shirt and pulled it over his head.

"I was thinking about grabbing some more clothes and bringing them over."

He said nothing else and seemed to be holding his breath. She knew he was asking permission. And usually she would panic right about now. Guys who wanted to spend more time with her made her uncomfortable. One date had tried to make brunch plans a week out, and she had freaked out. But, something about this just felt right.

She smiled. "Sure. Give me a couple of hours to calm the idiot down."

JT sighed and she heard it then. Pain filled the simple sound. For JT, he would rather die than hurt Anthony.

"Hey, he'll get over it. You know Anthony has a horrible temper."

He shook his head. "This was over the line. I knew…"

"What?"

"For the last few years it has been hard to ignore you."

She frowned. "What do you mean?"

He rolled his eyes. "Elena, you do know you're damned beautiful. And it was hard to ignore you."

Elena blinked. "Are you telling me you've been attracted to me for two years and didn't ask me out?"

He rolled his eyes. "It's against the code."

"What code?"

"I know you aren't stupid and you aren't deaf. I told you. Guys don't date their best friend's little sisters. It's not acceptable."

"But you are. Well, you're at least sleeping with me."

"Yeah."

"Do you regret it?" she asked, almost afraid of the answer.

"Not a chance," he said smiling. "I just think I lost Anthony as a friend."

"You haven't. Let me talk to him. And besides, you have me," she said taking his hand and pulling him closer. She kissed him gently, mindful of his split lip. "And that's more important than that idiot out there."

He shook his head. "I lost his trust."

"Don't worry about that. He'll get over it."

"What's taking so long?" Anthony practically bellowed from the living room.

"I'm going to kill him," she growled.

She led JT back out. Anthony was standing right on the edge of the kitchen, holding a towel to his nose. His shirt was splattered with blood, and he still looked like he wanted to start another fight with JT.

"I'll call," JT said.

"Okay."

He gave her a simple kiss, nodded toward Anthony and left.

The door clicked shut and silence filled the apartment. Then, Anthony exploded.

"What the hell, Elena?"

"What?"

She said as she walked back to her bedroom. She knew her idiot brother would follow her. It was the only way she could get him into the bathroom for her to clean him up. It only took a second before she heard his heavy footsteps behind her.

"You're sleeping with him? Or was it a one night

stand?"

"Let me look at your nose. You didn't clean it right."

He followed her into the bathroom.

"So, you slept with him?"

"I am not discussing my sex life with you. And you need to give JT a break."

"Why should I do that? Ow, dammit," he said when she started to clean out his nose.

"Stop cussing at me. Your language is atrocious. And quit being a whiner."

That shut him up. No Santini liked to be called a whiner. "Tell me why I should give him a break."

She shrugged. "I made the first move."

"Jesus, Elena." Disgust filled his voice.

"What?"

"I thought Mom raised you better than that."

"Oh, how very nineteenth century of you."

"You went after him? Like you attacked him? Mom would not approve."

She snorted. "Maybe you should have Mom tell you the real story on how she and Dad got together."

"What do you mean by that?"

She shook her head. "Ask Mom. She raised me to be like her. I went after what I wanted. What I have always wanted."

He said nothing as she finished cleaning his nose.

"So, this was last night?"

She shook her head. "No. We ended up together the weekend before he went UA."

He studied her for a second. Then understanding lit his eyes.

"That's why Mom was worried about you."

"What do you mean?"

"She's been fretting the last few weeks…since the wedding. She said you lost weight, that you'd been depressed."

"That's part of it. I also got a new commander."

"Who?"

"Dennis Vent."

Anthony made a face.

"Exactly. He hates having women in his squadron."

He frowned. "He's not giving you any problems, is he?"

"No, but if he was, I would take care of it myself, or go up through the command. I do not want you butting in. Either way, working for him is not fun. He doesn't do anything that would be considered bad, but you know what its like when your commander doesn't like you."

He blinked. "No. I don't."

She rolled her eyes. "Of course not. You are the legendary Anthony Santini. Everyone loves you—except your sister at the moment."

"Why did you have to mess around with JT?"

"I love him, Anthony."

He narrowed his eyes. "You have a crush. It'll pass."

"I love him. Sure it was a crush, but it's more now."

He sighed. "Dammit. Now I do have to kick his ass again."

"First of all, he kicked yours."

He made a rude sound. "It was a draw."

"You have a broken nose."

"He has a split lip."

"Either way, you will not go fight him. If you do, I will call Mom."

"And what, tell her I beat up the man who deflowered you?"

"Oh. My. God. JT did not *deflower* me. Have you been reading outdated romance novels? Good lord. You really do live in the nineteenth century."

"So you weren't a virgin. He still took advantage."

"I worked it so he would have to drive me home, then I had my hands all over him. He tried to leave me, but I jumped his bones."

He closed his eyes. "I did not hear that. I don't want to

know that."

He opened his eyes.

"But it's okay for one of your brothers to have sex? Me, I'm different?"

"Of course you are."

"Why?"

"You're my baby sister."

"You are horrible."

He shrugged. "Sorry, but I can't help it."

"Yes, you can. Grow up."

"Don't want to."

"I can't wait until some woman works you over. I will gladly give her insider information, because it is going to be so much fun to watch."

He followed her out of the bathroom. "What do you mean by that?"

"I have a feeling the woman who gets stuck with you is going to get you all wrapped around her finger. It is going to be enjoyable to watch."

He stopped her. "Hey, really. Are you okay with this?"

She looked at him and all of a sudden, he was the way she saw him when she was just a little girl. He was Anthony Santini, slayer of imaginary boogie men and the one person she could always count on. She blinked and realized she was getting misty-eyed.

"Are you crying?"

A thread of panic entered his voice. She always forgot that Anthony couldn't handle tears from anyone, especially her. She hoped he had a ton of little girls one day. It would be the perfect payback for using the term deflower.

"No. Just thinking about how you used to take care of me when I was little."

He shifted his weight from foot to foot and his face flushed.

"Oh, Anthony, I do love you."

She gave him a big hug, but whispered in his ear. "You mess with JT again, I *will* kick your ass."

CHAPTER THIRTEEN

Rage still poured through Anthony over an hour later. He couldn't believe that his best friend had slept with his baby sister. Never in his life had he been more surprised by a person. Of course, it didn't get past him that he was a trained investigator. Apparently he wasn't that good of an investigator if he had no idea that his best friend and little sister were involved. Anthony didn't care that he lived thousands of miles across the ocean. He should have picked up on it. Hell, he'd talked to both of them separately since JT had gotten back.

He scrubbed a hand over his face. Damn, he was tired. The flight he took had left late in the evening and landed in LA early that morning. He knew he had to talk to JT, but he thought it best not to go right now. First, he had to talk to Dante and figure out just what the hell he had been doing. Didn't he even know what his twin had been up to? Secondly, he was too exhausted to think clearly. He needed a shower and a meal. And some freaking sleep. He was too old for this shit.

He pulled up to the house Dante was renting with Madison. She had been living in it first and with her history of PTSD, it was best to keep put. It also helped that a Johnson lived next door. While not a Santini, they were the next best things, according to his Aunt Joey. He made his way to the door and knocked. It took a little longer than he expected for someone to answer it. He knocked again.

Finally, Dante answered. He was half dressed and looked like he'd just gotten out of bed. Jesus, everyone in his family was getting laid but him. At least, this one made sense since Dante was newly married and well…a Santini.

"Anthony?" Dante said as if still trying to figure out who the hell he was. "What are you doing here?"

"Mom asked me to check on Elena."

"So you flew from Hawaii to check up on Elena?" Dante still didn't ask him in.

"Dante, babe, let your brother in," Madison said from behind Dante.

Dante chuckled as he moved out of his way. "Sorry about that."

"I see that you married a woman too good for you. Just like I said at the wedding."

He stepped past his brother, who just rolled his eyes at him. Anthony ignored him. Instead, he gave his new sister-in-law a kiss on the cheek.

"I told you that you should run away with me."

She laughed. "It was already after we were legally married."

Her service dog Charlie sat on the floor beside her.

"Hey there, bud," Anthony said. Charlie's tail thumped on the floor.

"Not that we don't love having you here, but if you're supposed to be checking up on Elena, what are you doing here?" Madison said as she led him into the living room.

"I did go over there."

And everything went to shit after that. Just what the hell was he going to do about this?

"Did she punch you again?" Dante asked.

"What are you talking about?" Madison asked.

Dante sat down, then pulled her down onto the couch beside him.

"We were about ten and Anthony decided he needed to tell her just how to do things. Told her that a girl needed to just learn her place. See, Anthony thought that Elena, being the girl, should have to do the dishes every night. We were too manly. Elena hauled off and hit him in the nose."

She looked at Anthony. "She broke your nose."

"It wasn't a break," Anthony said.

Dante hooted. "Yeah it was. There was blood everywhere. And then he snuck up on her when she was raiding the fridge in the middle of the night. He came up behind her and grabbed her by the waist. She was sixteen by then, but it was just as embarrassing."

Dammit, his brothers loved telling that story. Elena was pretty damned proud of it too. Every time they wanted to embarrass him, they brought it up.

"It wasn't her. JT and I had a fight," he said.

Silence greeted that comment.

"Let me guess. You just showed up like you always did, no notice," Dante said.

"Yes."

"And she and JT were busy."

"No, ugh, don't make me think about it." Dante's comment suddenly hit Anthony. "Dammit, don't tell me that you knew about them?"

"Yeah."

"Since when?"

"Since the very first night."

The rage was back, mixed with a healthy dose of disbelief. "And you let it happen? What the hell, Dante?"

Dante shook his head. "Listen, my life with Elena is different than all of you. We had to go through high school together. Besides, she's a grown woman and she's not a virgin."

"But he's my best friend. Don't you think you should have told me?"

"I didn't know he was back until a day ago."

"But still, *fuck*, Dante."

Dante shook his head. "Listen, we had to go through

every horrible year together. By the time we both started dating, we agreed to stay out of each other's business. It was different for Carlos and Brando. They're both guys. Plus, they aren't as mean as Elena. So, yeah, I agreed to it. It was the only way to survive with my pride intact. Besides, I got the idea he was stupid in love with her."

Anthony had to bite back a growl. "I didn't ask."

"Of course you didn't. You just started fighting like you always do. You are one loud pain in the ass sometimes."

"Hey," he said turning toward Dante.

Madison stood. "Calm down, both of you." Charlie had come to stand beside her, and she patted the dog on the head.

He sighed. "Sorry, Madison." He didn't need to cause his sister-in-law to have an episode with her PTSD. She did well most of the time, but tension like this could be hard for her to take.

"You didn't ask JT how he felt?" she asked.

"I was too mad. He was walking down the hallway with nothing but a pair of boxers on; like they had just been in bed."

She cleared her throat, and he got the distinct impression she was trying not to laugh.

"What?" Anthony asked.

"Sorry. It's just funny. And since I have no siblings, I have no way to know how this all goes, but I am sure *you* didn't find it funny."

"No."

"It's rather sweet though. I know you care about her, but I have to believe that JT does too."

Anthony looked from her to Dante. "You said he was stupid over her?"

His brother nodded. "I get the idea that he got back in town, finished off the debriefings, then went straight to her apartment."

Anthony sighed. He couldn't seem to wrap his head

around the idea of his baby sister and his best friend having sex. Being in love was even worse. How was a man supposed to come to terms with that?

"So, he broke your nose?" Dante said. "Seems like the two of them were made for each other."

The doorbell rang.

"What the hell is this, Grand Central?" Anthony grumbled.

Madison went to the door. There was a murmur of voices, then more footsteps. Great, now someone decided to intrude.

Jack Johnson smiled. "Hey there, Anthony. How are things on the islands?"

"Great."

He looked at Dante. "Did I interrupt something?"

"Well, if you must know, Anthony here went over to Elena's unannounced. He discovered that his best friend and Elena are sleeping together and got into a fight. Much like his lover, JT apparently kicked his ass."

"Shut up, Dante," Anthony said, but there was little heat in the words now.

"I think you need some ice on that nose. It is really swelling up."

He wanted to say no, but he couldn't. Madison was too much of a sweetheart, and she just wanted to take care of him. Besides, if he stayed in the living room, there was a good chance he and Dante would start arguing again.

"Sure."

He followed her into the kitchen. She filled a soft ice bag up with ice, pulled out a mallet and smashed it. Charlie stood as if at attention, waiting to see if he was needed. Or, he might have wondered if there was food involved in this ritual.

She handed the ice bag to Anthony. "Be careful."

He set it on his nose and sighed.

"Come on over here and sit down."

She led him over to the kitchen table and sat him

down. “Did you take any pain meds?”

“No. Elena didn’t offer.”

She chuckled as she opened up the cupboard by the sink and pulled out a bottle of ibuprofen.

“You really can’t blame her. You did try to beat up her boyfriend.”

After filling up a glass of water, she gave him the pills then the water. Once he washed it down, she sat down on the chair beside his.

“I’m her brother.”

Madison shrugged. “Like I said, I can’t relate. Your family always overwhelmed me.”

“And you married into it?”

She gave him a blinding smile. “That should tell you how much I love your brother. It was hard to do, you know.”

“Love Dante? Yeah, he is a pain in the ass.”

She laughed. “No. Well, a little bit. Man always makes an embarrassing scene. But, what I am talking about is going from friends to lovers.”

He thought about that for a moment. Truth was, he had never had that issue. He rarely dated women he worked with or was friends with. “What made you do it?”

“Hard to describe what we went through earlier this year, but even if that hadn’t happened, I have a feeling Dante would have worn me down. It’s nice knowing that I just don’t love him, I like him too. That is really important.”

Madison had witnessed a murder and then been stalked by the man responsible. It had brought his brother and his new wife together faster, but she was probably telling the truth. Once a Santini man met the woman for him, he couldn’t think of anything else until he had her as his own. Anthony felt lucky to have escaped that particular problem.

“And I know she has had a crush on him for years,” Madison said. “I wasn’t sure who it was until I saw them together. When he's near her, she just lights up."

"Ugh, stop talking like that."

What he hated the most was that he just hadn't seen it. He should have seen it. Granted, she always seemed to tag along with them when she was a teenager, but that was nothing new. She had been following him around from the time she could walk, and he had always liked it. It had been embarrassing at the time, but, for a brief span of time, he had been her big hero brother. Now that he thought back though, he remembered there had been a few years she had completely ignored him. Sometime between grade school and the first time he brought JT home.

"That means he took advantage."

Madison snorted. "Really, Anthony, are we talking about the same woman? She saw an opening and took one last chance. Why do you think she's lost weight in the last few months? It was killing her that he was gone. I will tell you one thing. You better make it right, because I have a feeling that man loves her and wants more than just an affair. You are going to have to come to terms with it, or you will not only lose a best friend but also a sister."

He looked at the woman he now considered a sister, and felt nothing but happiness for his younger brother. She wasn't just gorgeous, but she was smart. Dante did a good job capturing the perfect woman for him.

"Tell me again why you're married to my idiot brother?'

"Hey," Dante yelled out from the living room. "Don't make me come in there and kick your ass, old man."

She shook her head. "Because another woman would be appalled that her husband just threatened his brother. I was made for him, just like I think Elena and JT were made for each other."

He made a face. "Do me a favor? Please stop saying that, at least for today. I need to get used to this situation."

"Sure thing. Want some coffee?"

"I would love a large cup of very black coffee."

She smiled and went to the cupboard. As she poured

his coffee, he realized he had to talk to his friend, but for the moment, he was going to sit back and spend time getting to know the woman who captured his brother's heart.

CHAPTER FOURTEEN

A few hours after he left Elena's apartment, JT heard the knock and knew without looking who it was. He'd been worried about this confrontation since he walked out of her apartment. He had wanted to stay and fight beside Elena, but he knew it would agitate the situation. Plus, Elena knew how to handle her own fights. Especially with her brothers. Prepared for another fight, he approached the door and opened it.

Anthony's nose was swollen and his eyes were turning black. Regret shifted through him. From the moment he met Anthony on the varsity Quantico team, they'd been friends. Not once had they had the kind of fight that brought them to fists.

Until Elena.

"Damn, I'm sorry."

Anthony's expression darkened. "I promise not to hit you if you invite me in."

JT stepped back and let his friend walk in. He shut the door as Anthony prowled the room. He knew when Anthony was in this kind of mood, it was best to let him keep moving. He'd never known a person who had to be moving constantly when he was thinking something out. If you tried to stop him, he exploded.

"Elena said I had to apologize to you." Every word was said from behind clenched teeth.

JT shoved his hands into the pockets of his jeans.

"Okay."

Anthony glanced at him and his frown turned darker. "I'm not going to."

"Okay."

Anthony stopped and turned to face him. "Dammit, quit being so damned reasonable."

Frustration marched down his spine. He could be understanding. Growing up in the Thomas house, he learned at an early age how to defuse a tense situation. But he didn't know what the hell to do in this case.

"What do you want from me, Anthony? I stepped over the line. I can understand."

"Shit." Anthony shook his head. "I don't want to admit when Elena was right."

"You're not making any sense."

Anthony paced away again, and looked out onto the patio. He shoved both hands through his hair. "I want to know why. Why Elena?"

There was enough confused irritation in his friend's voice, JT took pity on him. "She told you how it happened?"

"Yeah." He looked back over his shoulder at JT and rolled his eyes. "Of course she was the aggressor."

"She's a Santini."

"Why can't you just leave her alone? You were gone so long."

So, Elena had told him everything. "You would rather I just slept with her one night and never touched her again?"

"No." He turned again to face JT. "No, dammit. Why would you say that?"

"You're the one who said I was gone so long. How would you have felt if I had never called her again?"

"I would beat the shit out of you."

He threw his hands up in the air. "I can't win."

JT loved the man like a brother, but Anthony would make the most patient person want to throttle him. When Anthony was in this kind of mood, it was best to avoid him. Studying his friend's expression, JT knew that leaving him alone would not be an option.

He sighed. "You know that assignment was…bad."

Anthony nodded. The one person JT could share things about the job was Anthony. As another NCIS agent with the same security clearance, he could hear the things that most other people could not. He would also understand what undercover was like. Most people thought it was exciting. It had been, at first. Then, the last couple of years, it had gotten really old. A person couldn't live a true life pretending to be someone else.

"The only thing that kept me going was thinking about Elena."

Anthony settled his hands on his hips and frowned at him. "What are you telling me here, JT?"

JT drew in a deep breath then released it. "I love her, man."

The moment he said the words, JT realized just how important they were and how stupid it was to worry about saying them out loud.

"Aw, damn, why did you have to tell me that? Shit." He was quiet for a second. "Fuck me."

"What?"

"I can't beat the crap out of you again if you say things like that. You love her? How the hell did that happen?"

The confused irritation in his best friend's voice almost made him smile. He knew it had more to do with Anthony not being ready to accept that his sister had grown up.

JT shrugged. "Not sure. I just know I do."

"She's just a little girl."

"She's a woman, Anthony. You need to start accepting that."

He was quiet for a second as he continued to look out the window. "I still want to hit you."

"Get over it. Or at least work at getting over it. I really wanted you to be my best man."

For a second, Anthony didn't move, didn't say a word.

"You're planning on marrying her?"

JT nodded, warming up to the idea. He had known from the moment he touched her, he wanted her by his side and in his bed. Then he thought about the Santinis and their inability to keep secrets from each other.

"Don't tell her, because I think she's a little wary of getting married."

Anthony leveled his scariest Santini stare. "Can't you change your mind?"

JT shook his head. "I knew from that morning after. Really our first night together."

"The morning after?"

"We went to breakfast, and I sat beside her. It was the morning after Madison saw the murder. So, she wanted me to listen to what she said she saw and asked my advice."

Anthony nodded. "Makes sense."

"Yeah. Well, I was sitting beside Elena and in that instant I knew."

"You knew what?"

"I knew I wanted to be there beside her every day. I wanted to have breakfast with her and go to the beach. I wanted to do all kinds of things with her, and I wanted to share so much with her. I couldn't do anything at the time. I couldn't tell her I was in love with her and wanted to spend the rest of my life with her. It wouldn't be right."

"Because you were leaving." Anthony sighed. "Dammit."

"I would say I am sorry, but I can't be sorry. She's the best thing that has ever happened to me, besides being your friend."

"You're not good enough for her," Anthony grumbled as he crossed his arms.

"No one is."

Anthony made a sound of disgust. "Dammit, stop saying things like that." He paced away and looked out the window. "She told me you thought I wouldn't be your friend anymore."

JT held his breath, unsure of where Anthony was going with this. It was the one thing he would regret. But he couldn't give Elena up. Not now. Not ever.

Anthony studied him for a long moment. His face was expressionless. Then, he shook his head.

"I told you years ago, you were an honorary Santini."

The tension in his stomach loosened just a bit. "Guys aren't supposed to sleep with their friend's sister."

"But you love her. Did you know before?"

"I'm not sure. I think so or probably wouldn't have chanced losing you as a friend."

"And you love her now?"

"More than anything else in the world. She *is* my world."

"I can accept that, but stop talking like that. Damn, man, you're a Marine and an NCIS agent. I mean, man up."

He shook his head. "I can't help it. I know, it's insane, but I look at her and everything clicks. Everything can go wrong for me, but as long as I know she's there, I know it will all work out. She's the one I want to be with in the morning, at night, and until the day I draw my last breath."

Anthony groaned. "You're not even a Santini by blood, and you got struck with the curse. This is pretty damned bad."

"So, are we cool?" JT asked.

"We're getting there."

"I guess that is the best I can expect now."

"Now, the best thing you could do is offer me a beer."

Something else loosened in his chest. "I think I can help you with that."

Anthony followed JT to the kitchen. He grabbed a beer and handed it over to his friend. Anthony was looking at the papers on the table.

"What's up with that?"

"They think there might be another person in charge of the operation. I am going over everything to see if I can figure it out."

They sat down at the table. "So, Smith is a gopher?"

"Yeah. He is talking a deal with the prosecutor, so we think there is someone on top."

"Who was the commander?"

"Hickson. We couldn't believe he didn't know about it all going on under his nose, but there wasn't a connection. I mean, nothing. No records of money being transferred. No other contact between Smith and Hickson, other than what was to be expected. There was absolutely nothing to tie him to it. Which meant, he didn't know what the hell was going on under his nose. How the jackass made O-4, I have no idea."

"You know how it is sometimes. Hell, I know people with stars on their shoulders who don't know the first thing about commanding."

They both continued to look over the evidence. After another half hour, Anthony groaned.

"There's a pattern here that I can't seem to connect."

JT took a long draw on his beer. "Yeah, I agree. I wasn't satisfied, but the management was happy with it."

"Meaning, they wanted it to disappear as fast as possible."

He nodded. "You know how it is. They just want to put a lid on the scandal, but they want to put people away, so they at least look like they're doing their jobs."

Before Anthony could respond, JT's cell rang and he answered it when he noticed Elena's number.

"Hey."

"Hey, babe. Have you heard from Anthony?"

He glanced at the man in question. "He's right here."

She said nothing for a second or two. "He didn't hit you again, did he?"

"No. We're going over something for work."

"Hmm. Are you planning on spending all day with him?"

There was no annoyance in her voice, but he knew

something was bothering her.

"No. Don't you want to spend time with him?" he asked.

Anthony rolled his eyes.

"Not sure. He hit you, and I am still pissed about it. Plus, he used words like deflower and insinuated that I am not feminine. I really didn't like that."

JT chuckled and looked at Anthony. "Deflower?"

"Give me the phone," Anthony said, motioning with his hand.

"Anthony wants to talk to you."

She made a rude sound that was very much like the one her brother had made just moments earlier. "Anthony needs to learn when to butt the hell out. I just wanted to know what you were doing because Madison called and asked about getting together."

"Oh. Well, we'll probably go over this for the next few hours."

"Great. I don't know what is up with Mad, but she said she wanted some girl time."

"That sounds normal."

"Not for us. Really, when have you heard me use that term?"

He chuckled. "That's true."

"So, that's the reason I want to see her. I hope everything is okay."

"Did you want to talk to Anthony?" he asked again.

"Yeah, let me talk to the idiot."

He handed the phone to Anthony. He took it. "What do you want, runt?"

It was the name he had always called her when she was little.

"I have not threatened him again."

He listened for long moment.

"You would think you had some family loyalty. Your boyfriend can fight his own fights."

The word hit him then. *Boyfriend.* First, that told him

Anthony was getting used to the idea. Secondly, JT thought he was a little old for the term. And, the truth was, he wanted to be more than that. He wanted to be hers. Forever.

Anthony shook his head as he smiled. "I promise not to hurt him. Now go do girl things." More silence. "No, she seemed fine this morning. She took care of me since you kicked me out."

There was another long moment of silence as Anthony listened to Elena. There was a good chance he was getting yelled at again. "Okay. Do you want to talk to JT?" Then he said something in Spanish to her and handed the phone over to JT.

"Hey, there," he said.

"Okay, if he gives you any crap, beat the hell out of him and call Mom. I can't believe he's being such an ass."

"You're his little sister."

"I am not little."

"Wait, if I call your mom, then she's gonna know about us."

Elena sighed. "First, she probably already figured it out after talking to you the other night. Plus, if she didn't, one of the guys will tell her. They can't keep their mouths shut."

That much was true. Gossiping about each other was a full-time pastime in the extended Santini family. It was one of the things he loved about them. They might be kind of obnoxious about butting into each other's lives, but they did it out of love. "You're going out with Madison?"

"Yeah. I think we're doing a late lunch or something. And girl things. Whatever the hell that is."

"Be careful," he said as he watched Anthony roll his eyes.

"I will. You too."

Then she hung up.

"I can't believe I'm going to have to listen to that crap for the rest of our lives. Ugh."

"First, I have to convince her to marry me."

Suddenly, Anthony looked a little happier. "There is always a chance that she will say no."

"Thanks, for your vote of confidence."

Anthony shrugged. "Hey. I'm just telling you like it is. Besides, I figure if there's anyone who can keep up with her, it's you."

That was the closest thing he was going to get to an acceptance from Anthony. Happier now with the situation, he sat back down at the table and started to go over the evidence.

And sometime soon, he was going to have to have a talk with Elena—after he talked to her father first.

CHAPTER FIFTEEN

Elena sighed with happiness as she cut into the cheese enchilada and shoved it into her mouth. Cumin, red pepper, and cilantro danced over her taste buds a moment before the ooey gooey cheese hit her. She hummed in delight. She scooped up another bite. She wasn't delicate about it. When it came to food, Elena was never delicate.

"Hungry?" Madison asked with a chuckle.

"Yeah. For some reason I'm starving." She took another bite of enchilada. Damn, it was almost as good as her mother's, and that was saying a lot. Marcella Santini could cook anything Mexican or Italian.

"Having huge amounts of monkey sex will do that to you," Madison said with a chuckle.

Elena shared a smile with her friend. "Yeah, there is that. And it's been awhile since I've indulged."

"In sex or food?"

Elena laughed. "Both."

When Madison didn't say anything, Elena looked up at her. All of a sudden, her friend's face went pale. She sipped at water as if it were a fine whiskey.

"Is there something wrong?" Elena asked as she cut into her enchilada again.

Madison swallowed and shook her head. "Just a little queasy."

Charlie was sitting by her, relaxed. If she was

distressed, Charlie would have known it. He would be standing and pressed up against her legs.

"Do you have a fever?" she asked, feeling like a schmuck.

Thinking back on the day, she remembered Madison had been a bit lethargic. Neither of them were big shoppers, but Madison had petered out early. Elena realized her friend might be getting sick and she hadn't even noticed. She had been so self-involved, thinking about getting back to JT as soon as possible. She should have being paying attention to her friend.

Madison shook her head and closed her eyes. "No. Just like I said, a little queasy."

Elena studied her for a moment and then it all clicked. The lethargy, the queasiness, the pale skin added up to one thing. Even as it stunned her, joy filled her heart. Elena waited for Madison to open her eyes.

"You're pregnant," she said smiling.

Madison smiled and nodded.

"I am going to be an aunt," she said, letting out a hoot that drew a few stares, but Elena didn't care. She jumped out of her seat and hugged Madison. "This is fantastic news."

Madison hugged her back. Elena dropped into her seat. "How did Dante take it?"

"I thought he was going to pass out at first. Seriously, he was so pale. Afterwards, he started strutting around like he was some kind of stud."

Elena rolled her eyes. She had been around her four cousins during their wives' pregnancies, and they all had been horrible. "Good lord. He is going to be insufferable."

"He already is. He did tell your folks that he should get a medal for being first, or at least get your father's Harley."

Elena laughed. "He can try but Nando already called dibs on it. And you know how they treat the baby. When are you due?"

"March."

Elena started calculating it in her head, then she laughed. “Good thing y’all planned that wedding when you did. Close enough not to cause too much speculation.”

“There is that.”

Elena held up her margarita glass. “To the next generation of Santinis.”

Madison raised her water and clinked glasses with her.

“Now,” Elena said after taking a large gulp of her margarita, “what are our chances at getting another female into this mix?”

* * * *

Around two that afternoon, there was a knock at JT’s apartment door that had both he and Anthony frowning. He was going to ignore it, but there was always a chance it was Elena. He looked through the peephole and found another Santini standing on his doorstep.

He opened the door to a smiling Dante. “Hey, what are you doing here?”

“I was abandoned by my woman so she could spend time with Elena.”

JT stepped back. “We’re in the kitchen working.”

Dante followed him back.

“I see you two settled your differences,” he said, looking at Anthony.

“I don’t want to beat the shit out of him that much anymore,” Anthony said.

“According to Elena, JT beat you up.”

“Suck it, little brother.” But he didn’t really look up from what he was reading. Both of them had been working on it for hours, and now Anthony was as frustrated as JT.

Dante looked at the table then back up at JT. “What’s going on here and should I even be here?”

“The case is closed, so I guess it’s okay,” Anthony said.

“Cool.” He looked at their beers. “Got any more of

that?"

"Of course," JT said. "Fridge."

He sat back down at the table and Dante joined them.

They continued to work, but there was a hum of something coming off Dante. He seemed to be there for a reason, but it was as if he was avoiding the issue. Apparently, Anthony felt it too.

"Why don't you spit it out, Ant?" Anthony asked, using the nickname he'd given Dante when he was just a boy.

JT looked between the two of them, and he realized Dante had something to talk about. "I can leave if you need some privacy."

Dante shook his head. "You're family, JT. Plus, I have feeling, you'll officially be family before long."

He didn't see a reason to deny it and nodded.

"Freaking hell, just answer the question. We have work to do."

Anthony really didn't have a lot of patience.

"Madison's pregnant."

There was a second of stunned silence, then in true Santini fashion, Anthony let out a whoop. "Hot damn!"

He stood and pulled his brother out of the chair and gave him a hug. "Can't believe it." Anthony released his brother. "We should have something better than beer here."

"Naw, beer is better than any champagne we can afford," Dante said with a laugh.

JT shook his hand. "That's true. We should have cigars or something though."

Dante shook his head. "I come back smelling like that, there is a good chance Madison would barf on me. I can't take that again."

Anthony frowned and looked at his younger brother. "She seemed fine to me today."

"It hits her about lunch time, and it has more to do with smells than food. I have a feeling she won't want to go out much the next few months. Just a passing scent of something turns her green."

"Hey, why didn't you tell me this morning?"

"You were preoccupied. Plus, we had just found out the night before and we wanted to tell Mom and Dad and the Bakers first. We figured the grandparents had a right to know first."

He nodded then looked a little sick. "They are going to start harping on me again."

Dante laughed. "Don't worry, Anthony. It seems you're younger siblings have marriage and babies covered."

JT thought back to the ideas he had about having babies with Elena. Just thinking about watching her waddle around the house made him smile.

"Oh, lord, you've done it now, Dante. You have JT off in no man's land thinking about babies. Damn."

Dante laughed. "So, what are you two talking about here?"

"It's the job I just finished. The person we thought headed everything is talking a deal. Which means that he has something to deal with. So, I'm going over everything. There has to be something I missed."

"I have been over all the files too," Anthony said looking at him. "I can't find anything either. If it is there, it was well buried, so stop whining about it."

Dante laughed. "Want me to look over everything?"

Anthony looked at him then back to JT. "What do you think?"

JT thought it over. It wasn't exactly kosher and, like Anthony said, the investigation was over.

"Fresh eyes might help. Plus, he might pick up on something as active duty that we missed."

Anthony looked at his brother. "Okay, but you didn't see any of this. It's still considered classified."

"See what?" Dante asked as he took the file and started reading.

* * * *

It was well passed dinner time by the time Elena and Madison made it back to her apartment. They'd spent their afternoon window shopping for maternity clothes and baby furniture. It had been much more fun than anything girl centered like mani-pedis. At least for Elena.

She dialed JT's number wanting to check in and see what he was up to. Plus, she was worried that Anthony might have lost his temper again. JT could hold his own as he had proven that morning, but…

"Jethro's house of ill repute," Dante said.

"Hey, daddy," she said, laughing.

"Hey there, yourself. I take it Madison told you."

"Yeah. Well, she looked like she was going to barf, and I figured it out. Then we spent the afternoon shopping for things. I am going to spoil that kid like there is no tomorrow. And, yes, I am going to be the cool aunt, so expect me to buy things you disapprove of."

Dante chuckled. "I would be disappointed if you didn't."

The sound of his happiness made her happy. It was like that for all the Santinis, but for Dante and Elena, it was a little different. She was pretty sure it was the same way for Carlos and Brando.

"I'm so happy for you, bro."

"Thanks. Dad and Mom were thrilled."

"I bet they were. Aunt Joey's been giving her grief about being the only grandma of the bunch."

He chuckled. "Of course she was. What's up?"

"I called to talk to JT."

"We've been working."

She sighed. She had too many brothers. "Just put him on the phone, idiot."

The phone was jostled, and JT came on the line. "Hey, babe, what's up?"

"We just got back. If you're going to play NCIS with Anthony, we might watch some TV." She looked at

Madison, who nodded. "Yeah, that's what we're doing."

"Are you at Madison and Dante's?"

"No, we're at the apartment."

"Okay. We shouldn't be too long."

"No worries. We can entertain ourselves."

"Talk to you later," he said.

"Sure thing."

He hesitated then he said, "Bye."

"Bye."

She hung up the phone and frowned. JT was acting like something was wrong, or he wanted to talk about something.

"Something wrong?" Madison asked.

Elena pushed her thoughts aside. "Naw. Let's get you some tea and crackers and find something to watch."

"So," Madison said, as Elena went into the kitchen to put the kettle on, "what are the guys up to?"

"They're working on something for NCIS. I guess they dragged Dante into it."

"And that look on your face when you got off the phone?"

She could evade her friend, but she knew better than to hope for that. Looking at Madison she said, "Just a feeling when I got off the phone. Like JT wanted to tell me something."

"And that had you worried?" she asked. "Why?"

Elena grabbed the crackers and took them over to Madison. "I think one of the things that always stood in our way wasn't exactly a thing."

Madison nodded. "Anthony."

"I just worry with him back in the picture, no matter how temporarily, that he will cause JT to second guess his feelings."

"Oh, Elena, that man is not going to be second guessing anything. You don't have anything to worry about."

She shrugged. "I don't know what it was, but it just felt

like the wanted to tell me something."

Madison shook her head. "It's because it took you so long to hook up. Longer than it took Dante and me. So, you are going to end up seeing problems or worrying over things that just aren't that important."

Elena sighed and nodded. The tea kettle whistled and she hurried back into the kitchen. As she poured the hot water over the tea, she tried to push her worries away. JT didn't sound worried or upset as if he was going to be mean to her.

"Hey, do you want to watch some *Always Sunny*?" Madison asked as Elena walked back into the living area with the mugs of tea.

"Sounds good."

"Great, because Dante calls me horrible for loving this show."

"I don't know what you see in a man with no sense of humor."

Madison laughed and settled back against the sofa and sipped at her tea. She looked much better than she had earlier. At least, there was that. Charlie hopped up between the two of them on the sofa and laid down.

As they both enjoyed the antics of the Gang, she tried to push her worries about JT and second thoughts out of her head. There was one thing that was for sure.

If Jethro Francis Thomas thought she was going to let him walk away without a fight, he had another think coming.

CHAPTER SIXTEEN

A couple hours later, Elena made a couple more mugs of tea and joined Madison back in the living room.

"So, I have been meaning to ask you..." Madison said.

"What?" Elena asked, blowing on her tea.

"You and JT. Serious?"

Elena shrugged. Although she had tried to forget about the tone of his voice on the phone, it had never been far from her mind.

"For me, yes. For him, not sure."

Madison made a rude noise.

"What?" Elena said.

Madison stared at her for a long moment. "You're afraid."

Elena bristled. It might be a little true, but she didn't want to talk about it. "I am not."

Madison let one eyebrow rise up.

"Okay, maybe a little. Part of it is…I don't want to be too pushy."

Madison's face went comically blank. "You don't want to be too pushy? Wait." She looked around then leaned closer. "What have you done with the real Elena? Is this a body snatcher kind of deal where you took over her body? It would explain why she can eat the way she does and stays skinny."

Despite her worries, Elena chuckled. "Smartass."

"Hey, I have known you how many years? I have never known you to have an issue with being pushy. In fact, it is more of a motto for you."

"You make me sound horrible."

"No. I always admired you for it."

"Really?" Elena asked.

"I am not sure if I had a family as big as yours, I'd been able to compete for attention. They are intimidating to outsiders."

"I am what I am because of that."

Madison shook her head. "No. Sure, some of it is environment, but some of it is instinct. Why are you doubting it now?"

Elena rolled her eyes. "You know how it is when you fall in love. You worry the other person doesn't feel the same emotions, or at least, the same level of emotions. I just don't know."

Madison smiled. "Yeah, I do, but you can't doubt his feelings. Hell, he fought Anthony."

"That's true."

"And I saw him with you. Even before he left for the UA, he was falling for you. Honey, that man is completely in love with you."

Elena tried to control the happiness that spread through her. It would not do her any good to get all excited about something then have it fall it flat into her lap.

"You think?"

Madison nodded. "Dante said it today. He said he thought JT was stupid in love with you."

"He did?"

"Yep. It made Anthony gross out for a little bit."

She groaned. "Idiot. How am I related to these idiots? Seriously. If I wasn't Dante's twin, I would really wonder if they found me in a cabbage patch somewhere. And there are times I doubt we are twins."

"You two are too close not to be twins. And, be nice to Anthony. He's having a hard time coming to terms with the fact that you're a full grown woman."

She rolled her eyes. "Yeah. He used terms like *deflower*."

Madison choked on her water. "What?"

"Exactly. He wanted to fight for my honor because apparently being a Marine pilot doesn't mean I can take care of myself. He went all caveman on me and acted like I'd been ravaged by JT."

"Well…" Madison said. Then they both laughed.

"Okay. That happened, but it had more to do with me taking charge."

"What do you think your parents will say?"

She shrugged. "Not sure, but Mom adores him. And she talked to him the other night."

"Really?"

"Yeah, I was on the phone with her when he walked in. I have a feeling she knows what is going on. She didn't ask to speak to me again. Of course, I am not sure JT would allow that."

"Why would you say that?"

"I was undressing him."

"While he was on the phone with your mother?"

Elena laughed. "Yeah. And thinking about it now, I did it when he was on the phone with Anthony before JT left on his last assignment."

Madison shook her head. "You truly have a sick sense of humor."

"Kind of hard not to have it when I grew up with that idiot bunch of brothers."

Madison blinked and all of a sudden tears appeared in her eyes. Panic set in. She could handle tears, but she couldn't handle Madison Baker Santini in tears.

"What did I say?" she asked, worried she had said something to hurt her feelings.

"Nothing, really."

Elena handed her a box of tissues.

"Thank you. The crying is worse than the icky stomach. I swear, I cried during a commercial the other day."

"Was it one of those animal shelter commercials? Those are designed to make you cry. It's sick.

She shook her head and blew her nose rather loudly. "No. It was a commercial for Olive Garden."

Elena blinked. "You cried over Italian food?"

"Well, not the food. I thought about how I love pasta and how Dante makes it for me when I ask. Then, all I could think of was him cooking in the kitchen and me sitting there holding a little miniature version of him. I just burst into tears."

"Ah, okay. Do me a favor?"

"What?" Madison asked sniffling into her tissue.

"Do that in front of Anthony. He really has panic attacks over crying, and I want to get it recorded and onto YouTube."

* * * *

Three hours later, JT was just as irritated with the case as when they started. No, he was even more irritated. He was fucking furious. He knew there was something about the case that had been bothering him, but he had wanted to get back to Elena. Another reason to walk away from undercover work.

"Hey, don't take it so hard. I don't think I would have seen it either," Anthony said.

He grunted. "I got impatient."

"You got impatient?" Anthony asked in disbelief.

Dante studied them for a moment or two. "Am I missing something?"

He didn't respond because he was still reprimanding himself for rushing the investigation.

Anthony took over the explanation. "JT has a reputation…well, it goes back to the Marines. He has the patience of a saint. No matter the task, he would spend all his time on it to get it done right."

Anthony gave him a look, and he knew what his friend was remembering. JT had so much patience because of his father.

"And you didn't have it for this case?" Dante asked.

He got up and paced away, angry with himself and angry with the situation.

"I'll be damned. You were telling the truth," Anthony muttered.

He glanced at his friend. "Of course, I was telling the truth. And it was so damned frustrating. Every time I opened one line of investigation, another one would pop up. Like a fucking hydra that just wouldn't die. And all I wanted to do was come back here."

"And so, when it looked like this captain was guilty, you accepted it."

There was no recrimination in Dante's voice, but he didn't understand the work like Anthony did. It made him sloppy, and that was one reason he knew he couldn't do UA anymore. At least not for awhile.

"I should have looked closer."

"The perfect Jethro Thomas made a mistake. Oh no, we might think you're human," Anthony said, not trying to hide his sarcasm. "Get over yourself and think. You know there is something you're missing, and you know this case better than anyone."

He started to turn the evidence over in his head when his cell rang. Dammit, but when he saw Elena's picture on the screen, his irritation dissolved a bit.

"Hey there."

"Whatcha doing, Jethro?"

"We're still working the case." He glanced at the clock and realized it had gotten late. Hell, it was dark outside. He walked away from her brothers into his living room. "Sorry, time just got away from us."

"No, worries, just wanted to check on ya. We'll

entertain ourselves."

"Listen, Elena…" He stopped talking when he realized he didn't know how to tell her he loved her. Of course, doing it on the phone was kind of tacky and kind of cowardly.

"What?"

He sighed. "We need to have a talk."

Silence. "A talk?"

Her voice sounded funny. All the warmth had drained from it. In fact, she sounded icy. He wasn't sure if he had ever heard that in her voice.

"Yeah, a serious talk."

She said nothing for a second or two. "Not over the phone."

"We could talk on the phone."

And there was something niggling in the back of his head, telling him to blurt out just how he felt.

"No. Not on the phone."

Her voice was distant. Odd.

"Okay. But we *will* talk."

"Sure. Call me when you're done."

Then she hung up. He frowned and clicked his phone off.

"Trouble in paradise?" Dante asked, from behind him. Of course he was there. The Santinis had no trouble eavesdropping. Hell, they were proud of it and saw it as part of being a close family.

He looked at Elena's twin. "Not sure."

"Want some advice?"

His pride shouted no, but his heart knew if one man knew Elena, it was this one.

JT nodded.

"Be up front and don't dance around the subject. Elena does better with fact and straight talk."

"I tried."

"If you're going to tell Elena you love her, you need to tell her in person."

He studied Dante for a moment longer and nodded again. "Gotcha. Where's Anthony?"

"He was talking to a friend he has stationed at Twentynine Palms. He was checking up on a few things. He said he had a feeling about something."

Dante rolled his eyes, but JT didn't doubt his best friend. He had an eerie sixth sense when it came to hunches. MCAGcc was where his investigation had been and if Anthony knew someone there, he or she would know what the hell was going on.

The man in question just walked through into the living room. His frown was almost as dark as when he found JT at Elena's.

"What's up?" JT asked.

"Hickson went AWOL."

"Hickson?"

"Yeah. And, I just got off the phone with Glover. He said he finally got to talk to Smith about the deal. He wanted his family safe because Hickson doesn't go after people straight forward."

"What are you talking about?"

"Hickson is apparently a real bastard. He doesn't deal with the person he feels wronged him. He takes whoever is important to that person and kills them, or at least tries to. If anything, he terrorizes the family members or significant others. On top of that, the man was out of his mind when you blew his operation. He apparently sent Smith's wife quite a few threatening texts. Hickson wants revenge."

Something tickled at the back of his throat. His stomach churned.

"So, this Captain Smith turned evidence in exchange for keeping his wife safe?" Dante asked.

Anthony nodded. "She's pregnant. Top it off, Smith apparently had no way of saying no to the Major. He bullied and threatened people who worked for him. He was a year away from retiring and disappearing with millions. They were going over all the information and realized there was some kind of scheme at the last three bases the bastard was stationed at.

"Fuck me," JT said as he rubbed the back of his neck. "How did we all miss it?"

"He played the perfect Marine. Plus, he didn't go after big assignments, and he always got someone to do the dirty work for him, someone down the line in his chain of command. He did a good job, and they thought he kept his nose clean," Anthony said.

"And, think about it, JT," Dante commented. "Other Marines won't see him as a threat. I know I wouldn't. There are so many people competing for fewer and fewer assignments. So, if there is one guy who is just looking to get the safe job that will ensure his twenty years, another person would dismiss him. No ambition for making higher rank doesn't mean the bastard wasn't ambitious."

Anthony drew his attention. "Worse, because he was the supervisor and had been ruled out, he saw the case file. And even worse, the man knows you were working undercover."

"What?" JT asked, panic fluttering in his chest.

"Apparently, someone from NCIS let it slip to his commander. It was mentioned that he might have your name."

Everything started to fall into place. Horror hit him first, then terror.

"Fuck." JT grabbed his keys and started dialing Elena again.

"What?" Anthony said as Dante and he followed JT out of the door.

"There is one person who would stand out to Hickson if he was casing me. I have spent every day with Elena since I returned."

Elena wasn't answering her phone. Dammit. The woman picked this one time to ignore his calls or not be in range. Or…he didn't want to think about *or*.

"You think he would go after her," Anthony said as he

headed to JT's truck.

He nodded and opened the driver's side door. Anthony followed him, pushing him over. JT frowned at him, and he frowned back.

"What are you doing?"

"Driving. You wouldn't be able to keep your mind on the road. Plus, you can keep calling Elena."

"I'll try to call Madison too," Dante said as he settled in beside JT.

He hit redial on his phone again, hoping that she was just mad. His worry increased with each ring. Damn the woman for being so stubborn. He hung up and hit redial again as Anthony swerved around a slow minivan.

No answer. Still going to voicemail. His panic turned into terror as Anthony pressed harder on the gas, breaking more than a few laws to get to Elena and Madison.

JT prayed they would get there in time, or he might not have a reason to live.

CHAPTER SEVENTEEN

Elena ignored the buzzing of her phone as she paced the living room. She was so irritated with JT at the moment, she wanted to scream, but she wouldn't. And she couldn't talk to him. Not right now. If she did, there was a good chance she would insult him.

Anthony wasn't the only Santini with a temper.

"Hey," Madison said as she and Charlie returned from the bathroom. She watched her pace for a few moments. "What's up?"

"Nothing."

Idiot man. Spends one day with her brother, and he starts having second thoughts. And, it was definitely her brother's fault. He deserved some of her anger. Most of it. JT had just been getting used to them as a couple. Anthony shows up and makes him feel guilty or that he stepped over some kind of line. Or something.

"Um, you're pacing the floor."

"I'm in love with a dumbass."

Madison said nothing as she watched her. Both Charlie and Madison moved their heads back and forth. They looked like they were at tennis match.

"Ugh, you're making me sick to my stomach," Madison said as she sat on the couch. "What has you upset, and why do you believe you're in love with a dumbass?"

"He tried to cool it off on the phone. Wanted to tell me something."

"How do you know it was that he wanted to cool it off? Did he say that?"

"No. He eluded to it."

Madison shook her head. "I think you are assuming, and that is never good." Madison's phone went off. "Dante."

Before Elena could tell her friend to ignore her husband, Madison clicked it on. "Hey, babe."

Almost at the same time, the doorbell rang. Irritated, she stomped to the door.

She could barely hear her friend talk, as she had walked back into the bedroom for some privacy. She looked through the peephole and found a man dressed in a Marine uniform on the other side. A major, one she didn't know.

"Whoa, slow down, Dante," Madison was saying as she walked back out into the living room. "You're not making any sense. A major is after Elena, why?"

Right then, something turned in her stomach. She swallowed as icy fear slid down her spine. She knew something was very, very wrong.

"Madison, go into my bedroom with Charlie, lock the door, then go into the bathroom and do the same."

"What?" Madison said.

"Call 911 and tell them there is a dangerous man at the door, a Marine."

She could hear Dante on the other end of the line jabbering away. There was no longer polite knocking on the door. That was good. If the bastard wanted to draw attention to himself, she was okay with that. It would draw attention to the situation, and more people would call for help.

As she thought about their options, she knew she had to get Madison as far away from whoever was on the other side of the door. Elena took the phone from Madison as the pounding on the door increased. "Dante, are you on your way over?"

"Yes."

"Okay, Madison will be safe, but hurry." Elena handed the phone back over to Madison. "Here, take mine, call 911 on there, keep the line open with Dante."

"I can help you. I'm not unable to fight now." She knew her friend was talking about her PTSD.

Elena shook her head. "You're pregnant. You need to make sure you keep you and that baby safe."

Madison wasn't about to give up. "Come with me. We'll be safer together."

"No. If he has no one to get his attention, he will have more time to get to you." A threatening growl rumbled in Charlie's chest. Elena didn't think she had ever heard the companion pet sound so threatening. "I can handle the asshole until the guys get here. Go."

Madison nodded as she did Elena's bidding. The sun had set, so Elena turned off the lights. The major was pounding harder and muttering under his breath. She couldn't make out the words, but it didn't sound good at all.

The door blew open, bringing the Major with it.

"Elena Santini, I am here to help you."

So, maybe he was some kind of demented mental patient. No one would bust through a door like that and announce he was there to help her. There was something definitely off about the guy. She crouched down on the other side of the couch. From what she saw of the intruder, he outweighed her by quite a bit.

"I was sent by Jethro Thomas. He's a friend of mine."

Lie. That was easy. No one called him Jethro but her mother. She did sometimes, but it wasn't something a friend would call him. Everyone who worked with him called him Agent Thomas or JT.

"There was a problem with his last case."

And she was pretty sure the bastard now moving toward the bedroom door was the problem. He started messing with the doorknob. With his back turned in her direction, she decided to get a good look at him. She inched out, trying her best not to alert him of her location.

First thing she noticed was that the man was a mess. He had his uniform on, but no self-respecting Marine officer would look like that, at least not outside a war zone. It hadn't been washed in a few days. Twigs hung from the sleeves, and he wasn't wearing a cover. A sure sign there was something very, very wrong with the man.

He stepped back from the door, and she saw his hand raise up as if shoot the doorknob. Damn.

She rose up and came at him. He turned with an almost comical surprised look on his face. She used as much force as she could as she brought her hand down on his arm. It had the desired effect. He dropped the gun. She didn't stop her forward motion. Elena slammed into the man, sending them both tumbling to the ground.

"Bitch," he screamed.

She ended up on top and had the advantage of being able to untangle herself from the major. She was up and on her feet, moving away from the bedroom door and toward the entrance to her apartment. If she could lead him out of the apartment, that would mean he would be moving away from Madison. Plus, outside, there were people. People meant witnesses.

Her hopes were dashed the moment she felt his fingers wrapping around her ankle. With a jerk of his hand, he brought her down on the ground. Her head smacked hard against the foyer floor. She blinked as stars appeared in front of her eyes. Pain radiated from the spot that got the brunt of the hit on the floor. It was so strong she almost vomited.

I have never met such a pain in the ass as you. Why didn't you just go off the road?"

He seemed to be talking to himself. He continued

muttering, but she couldn't make out the words after that one. Suddenly, what he said hit her. He was the bastard who ran her off the road. He still had his slimy fingers wrapped around her ankle. She pulled her foot back and smacked him in the face. Twice. The crack of bone filled the apartment. Blood spurted from his nose as he screamed. Still, he didn't let go of her leg. She pulled her leg back to hit him again, but he swung his free arm around and she saw the gun.

She froze, her blood turning to ice. All the air backed up in her lungs as terror wound through her system. Elena stifled the scream that was lodged in her throat. She was worried that if Madison thought she was in trouble, she would come out. The guys should be there within a minute to two, depending on when they had actually left.

"Yeah, I thought that might get you under control."

She would not let him shoot her. Not now. Not at this point in her life. She had no idea who he was, but she did know that he wanted her dead. Fuck it. She would not take this lying down.

Using what little strength she had left, she reared up and head butted the man. They tumbled back together, and the gun went flying out of his hand again. This time, she straddled his chest and punched him in the face. He was already bloody, and her hit to his nose just made it worse. She was still hitting him when she heard JT shout behind her.

"Bastard," he roared. He came rushing behind her. Hands were on her, and she realized they were Anthony's. As he pulled her away, JT grabbed the man who had attacked her.

"Where are you hurt?" Anthony demanded as he picked her up.

Dante was pounding on the bedroom door yelling out Madison's name.

"I'm not hurt. Not really. Get JT off the man."

Anthony set her on her feet and looked her in the eye.

Apparently deciding she was okay, he yelled out, "JT, I think the blood is his."

JT stopped in mid-punch, and his head whipped around. This was not the man she knew. His face was a mask of anger, and his eyes were filled with murderous intent. He stood and came to her, pulling her against his chest. She heard Dante talking to Madison and Charlie, and she sighed with relief.

Sirens sounded in the distance.

"I can't breathe," she said, telling the truth. All of a sudden, the room seemed to be spinning. Her head was throbbing.

He gave her some space. "All the blood is his?"

She nodded, then felt another roll of nausea turn over in her stomach. She swallowed and tried to keep herself from throwing up.

"There's blood on the back of your head," Madison said from behind her.

She turned to face her, and the room spun so fast she faltered.

"I think you need a doctor," JT said, but he sounded like he was in a tunnel far away. When did he get so far away?

She shook her head, which was a mistake. She swallowed the rise of bile that clogged her throat. "No."

JT opened his mouth to argue with her, and she just couldn't take it. She bent over and threw up on his shoes.

CHAPTER EIGHTEEN

Hours later, after the police had left her apartment, and the EMT's had told her she had a slight concussion and really should go to the hospital, she found herself in JT's bedroom. Unfortunately, she wasn't alone. Santinis filled the room. Sure, it was just two brothers and a sister-in-law. Worse, she knew her parents were on their way. She had told them not to come when Dante had called, but they apparently had been planning a trip to see them.

She sighed as she looked around the room. Dante was sitting in the chair beside the bed, Madison on his lap. Anthony had been brooding in the corner since she'd gotten there. And JT, well he sat beside her on the bed not saying much. With Santinis, they took double the energy to deal with. On a normal day, they were difficult to handle. At five-thirty in the morning after being attacked by a crazed O-4, she just wasn't in the mood to deal with them. Add in the fact that her head was still throbbing, and she didn't have the patience. She loved her family, but they were driving her up the wall. Besides, she had something she wanted to discuss with the dumbass she was in love with.

"Everyone out. Go away."

Anthony frowned. "But, the EMT said you needed to stay awake."

"I think we should leave," Madison said.

Elena tried to offer her friend a smile, but she found it hard. Any movement made her head pound even more. She'd kill to have the lights out, but Anthony had deemed it unadvisable since he felt she needed to stay awake. Idiot.

Elena studied her friend. She looked well, but there were dark smudges beneath her eyes and she was still pale. Charlie hadn't left her side since the incident. She was relieved that Madison was fine and hadn't had an episode because of the stress of the night.

"Dante, take her home. She needs her rest."

That was true. She didn't know who had slept that night. Probably no one. The sun was coming up, and her friend looked ready to drop.

"We want to be here," Anthony said.

She cut him a look. "Seriously, leave."

Apparently, the look and the tone of her voice got to him.

"Come on," Madison said to him. "You can tell me more horrible stories about my husband."

He sighed and leaned over the bed and gave her a kiss on the forehead.

"Give him hell," he whispered just loud enough for her to hear. It was probably as close to a blessing as she was going to get from Anthony. He had accepted the fact that they were involved.

Elena nodded and watched as he stepped out of the room with Madison. Dante kissed her in the same fashion.

"Don't do shit like that again," he said gruffly.

"What, save your wife and child?"

He sighed dramatically. "Damn, I am never going to be able to live this down. You'll be bringing it up forever."

She motioned to him to come closer, then she set her hand on his, which rested on the bed beside her.

"What hurts you wounds me."

It was something their mother had always said, but for Dante and Elena, it had a special meaning. He nodded, apparently unable to speak. He gave JT a look.

"I almost feel sorry for you."

She rolled her eyes. "Go away, butthead."

He was laughing as the door closed. She looked at JT then.

"So, you want to be a coward?"

His eyes widened, then they narrowed. "Be careful the way you throw that word around."

"What can I call you? You were going to leave me."

His frown darkened. "Where in the world did you get such a dumbass idea as that?"

"You said you had something to talk about. It was definitely about us. And it was important. It happened just when Anthony showed up. So, you are a coward. You would rather throw what we have away so you can keep Anthony as your friend."

Anger moved over his features and for the first time, she realized she might have misunderstood what he had been trying to say. She swallowed, but she refused to back down. She was going to fight him tooth and nail.

"I wasn't trying to break up," he said, rage practically dripping from every word. "You stopped me and I agreed not to talk over the phone. Where did you get the idea that I wanted to break up with you? That's just stupid."

"I thought…"

Her words trailed off as he loomed over her. "You stopped me because you were afraid. *You*, not me, were the coward."

"That's not true." *It wasn't, was it?* "Okay, I was afraid you were going to use your friendship with Anthony to drive a wedge between us."

"When have I done that with anything?"

She frowned. "Always."

"No. I avoided you because you were my best friend's little sister and off limits. But from the moment we slept together, tell me who is the one who was trying to keep from being found out? Who is the one who wanted to keep our relationship a secret?"

"I didn't want them nosing in."

"Yeah? Well, why not?"

"Because I love you, dumbass. I wanted you all to myself so you could figure how perfect we were together."

He blinked. "You really are stupid. Jesus, Elena, from the moment we slept together, I have been at your side. You can't count my assignment."

She would never do that. Duty was something almost sacred to a Santini. "I don't."

He sighed. "Why do you think I requested a break from UA's?"

"You asked…"

Hope filled her heart as she felt something heavy lift off her soul.

"Yes. I couldn't keep doing that. First, I'm getting too damned old for that. And secondly, when you find the person you want to spend the rest of your life with, you don't want to waste time pretending to be someone else."

She struggled to sit up, and he was by her side in a minute to help. "Be careful."

It came out as an order, and she slanted him a dirty look. He gave her one right back.

"You better change that attitude right now, woman. I can be mean with you because of the risk you took."

"I didn't have a choice."

"You could have hidden from him."

"Would you ask one of my brothers to do that?"

"Of course not."

"Sexist," she spat out.

"No. When the woman I love is in danger, I have the right to want you safe."

"I couldn't hide with her. She needed to stay away from him. With her condition—besides the PTSD—I couldn't let her become a target. You would have done the same thing."

And she was happy to have known about it. If not, she

probably wouldn't have been such a bitch and insisted that her friend go hide. She had used it against Madison, and she would do it again in a heartbeat.

"So, how badly was he hurt?" she asked.

"He'll survive."

"You won't be brought up on charges?"

"He was attacking you. What kind of asinine comment is that?"

"Well, maybe I want to make sure you aren't going to jail, you dumbass."

"Why would I be going to jail? You're the one who beat the shit out of him. And, I am getting sick of being called a dumbass."

"Then stop acting like one."

He growled and paced away. "I used to have an easy life. Sure, people would shoot at me, and I had to hang out with scum who shouldn't be able to walk free, but now…"

"What?" she asked when he didn't continue.

He stopped walking and frowned down at her. "*You* are a pain in my ass."

JT looked at the woman he loved and waited for her to yell at him. He shouldn't have said what he did, but he was so frustrated. In less than eight hours, he had been more terrified than he had in his entire career in the military and NCIS. He'd gotten shot three times during his adulthood and right now, he couldn't remember the deep bone fear of those events. When he realized that Hickson knew were Elena was, and he was on his way to make JT pay for ruining his scheme, the fear that almost stopped his heart is something he would remember until the day he died.

Then, in a split second, she surprised him. Elena Michon Santini—the girl who never cried, even when she broke her arm in the seventh grade—burst into tears. And not just little tears. Big, sloppy tears and loud sobs. Wailing. He was sure he'd never seen anyone wail like her. The door burst open, and Anthony was frowning at him.

JT held up his hands.

"What the hell is going on in here?" he growled.

JT shook his head. "I don't know. She just started doing it."

Anthony looked at Elena, then him. "Well, make it stop."

He opened his mouth to tell him he didn't know what to do, but Elena took care of it.

"Go get bent, Anthony," Elena said.

Anthony studied her for a second, then he gave JT a nasty look of warning before he slammed the door shut.

"Mom always says Anthony was born in a barn." On that, she drew in a long, shuddering breath and looked down at her comforter. "I'm sorry. I didn't mean to start crying like that and don't mean to be a pain in the ass."

"I shouldn't have said it."

"Why not? It's true."

He couldn't lie and tell her she wasn't. Elena was one of the most self-possessed people he knew. She understood her faults. And he loved every last one of them even when she was being a pain in the ass.

"It doesn't mean I don't love you."

"I thought you wanted to end everything. You sounded so definite on the phone, so I thought you decided not to be with me." Her voice was so soft, and he knew she was ashamed. He knew her well enough to understand she was embarrassed by her vulnerabilities.

He settled on the bed beside her. "I had made a decision. I can't believe you thought I was thinking of breaking it off with you. I don't know where you get those insane ideas."

She rolled her eyes. "I'm not an easy woman to live with. Ask any of my brothers. I'm difficult."

"You're an acquired taste."

She rolled her eyes. "That sounds like a line from a movie, Jethro."

He chuckled. "It's true. Besides, I don't want easy. I'm

a Marine and an NCIS agent. Easy is boring as hell. I want pushy. I want a woman who kicks my ass when I need it. And I am pretty sure that's you. I need you beside me at night and I need you to need me."

She blinked as her eyes filled up with tears. "Oh, my."

"Exactly. I've been walking around with that in my heart for months now. I knew the moment I touched you that God had made you for me. I just had to figure it all out."

"What took you so long?"

"First some idiot thought we shouldn't say anything to her family. Second, I really didn't want to say anything to you until I talked to your father and Anthony about it."

"Why would you want to talk to them?" she asked as he grabbed a tissue and wiped away her tears.

"I felt I needed their permission to ask you to marry me. I think Anthony already had an idea."

"Marry you?" she asked, her voice a little stronger.

"Yeah," he said, entwining his fingers with hers.

"Why would you need to talk to them?"

This was the hard part, because whenever he spoke of his connection to Anthony and her father…it was just difficult to express.

"My father is a bastard. You know that. Everyone knows that."

She was blessedly silent for once and just nodded.

"Your father took me in as one of his own sons and treated me like part of the family. Your mother thinks of me as her son in a way. Before meeting them, I was never accepted for just being me. All of you gave me that."

"She tells people she has six sons and one daughter."

He smiled. "I had a bit of a crush on her when I first met her."

She laughed. "Figures. I get my mom's cast offs."

He cupped her face. "I had to show them all respect. I needed them to know that I love you more than life, and where ever you go, I go."

She didn't say anything for a moment, then she shook her head. "I can't expect you to give up your career."

"We'll figure it out. I just wanted them to know how much I respected you, and how proud I would be to be your husband. I want you flying in that uniform, because I know it is part of you. I love that part, along with the one that seems to think she needs fifteen little doodads on her keychain."

"Yeah?" she asked.

He nodded. "Plus, like I told you. You are pretty damned hot in your uniform. But I need to ask your father's permission first."

Then she motioned with her head behind him. "You can tell them now."

He looked over his shoulder and realized her parents were standing there. Her mother was dabbing at her eyes with a tissue, and her father was smiling.

"Sorry," Tony said. "We'll let you two have a moment alone."

He ushered his wife out and shut the door.

JT closed his eyes and turned around to Elena. Of all of the asinine...when he opened them, he found her smiling at him.

"I can't believe I screwed that up."

"How did you screw it up? They looked pretty happy to me."

"Your mother was crying."

"Happy tears. You know Mom. If she gets sad, she gets pissed."

He sighed because that much was true.

She said nothing else, but she kept smiling at him.

"What?"

"When do I get this amazing proposal?"

"I need to get a ring."

"You need a ring? You were going to propose to me without a ring? That's kind of tacky," she said in an overly prissy voice.

"I take it back. I am not going to propose, we'll just get married."

Elena smiled. "I have to say, you do know how to make a Santini woman happy."

He shook his head. "You're crazy. All of you."

She pulled him closer. "Yeah, and you're one of us. Plus, you just said you wanted to marry me, so our blood will be mingled with our children."

He brushed his mouth over hers but said nothing.

"Please tell me you want to have kids," she said.

"Oh, yeah," he said as he leaned her back. "I think we can definitely have as many kids as you want."

He brushed his mouth over hers again. He needed this connection, to know that she was okay.

"Please, don't ever do that again," he said.

"What?"

"Be in danger."

She laughed. "Oh, babe, you're in so much trouble. You're marrying a Marine."

With that announcement, she pulled his head back down. He was seriously thinking about stripping her clothes off her when there was pounding at the door.

"I might say I am okay with this, but it doesn't mean I don't expect you two to behave while I'm here," her father said from the other side of the door.

She made that rude sound he loved so much. "I am going to kill him. In fact, I might kill him, then use his body to kill Anthony."

JT chuckled and set his forehead against hers. "I love you, Elena."

"I love you, too."

He kissed her and was losing himself again when her father knocked on the door again.

"I'm really not kidding."

"They don't listen at all," Anthony said loud enough for them to hear.

"Oh, Anthony, don't be a tattletale. No one likes

those," Mrs. Santini said.

"They're discussing us as if we aren't here," he said, shaking his head.

"It will only get worse but you're stuck now."

"More than happy to be stuck with you," he said as he bent his head to kiss her again. He ignored the rather loud argument her family was having on the other side of the door and went about celebrating his engagement.

ABOUT THE AUTHOR

From an early age, USA Today Bestselling author Melissa Schroeder loved to read. First, it was the books her mother read to her including her two favorites, Winnie the Pooh and the Beatrix Potter books. She cut her preteen teeth on Trixie Belden and read and reviewed To Kill a Mockingbird in middle school. It wasn't until she was in college that she tried to write her first stories, which were full of angst and pain, and really not that fun to read or write. After trying several different genres, she found romance in a Linda Howard book.

Since the publication of her first book in 2004, Melissa has had close to fifty romances published. She writes in genres from historical suspense to modern day erotic romance to futuristics and paranormals. Included in those releases is the bestselling Harmless series. In 2011, Melissa branched out into self-publishing with A Little Harmless

Submission and the popular military spinoff, Infatuation: A Little Harmless Military Romance. Along the way she has garnered an epic nomination, a multitude of reviewer's recommended reads, over five Capa nods from TRS, three nominations for AAD Bookies and regularly tops the bestseller lists on Amazon and Barnes & Noble. She made the USA Today Bestseller list for the first time with her anthology The Santinis.

Since she was a military brat, she vowed never to marry military. Alas, fate always has her way with mortals. Her husband just retired from the AF after 20 years, and together they have their own military brats, two girls, and two adopted dog daughters, and is happy she picks where they live now.

You can keep up with Mel all over the web:
www.MelissaSchroeder.net
Twitter.com/Melschroeder
Facebook.com/MelissaSchroederFanpage
Facebook.com/TheSantinis
www.facebook.com/groups/harmlesslovers-Mel's Harmless Addicts Fangroup

Join Mel's Newsletter to keep up with releases, sales, and appearances.

http://eepurl.com/N2iob

Coming in the Fall of 2015, Harmless is getting an exciting new spinoff series! Look for an announcement coming in March, but to make sure you are one of the first to know, join Mel's Newsletter or join The Harmless Addicts! She will make the announcement there!

Don't miss Elena's twin, Dante, in A Santini in Love, now available everywhere!

She was the last woman standing.

Madison Baker was born and bred to be a Marine. When a roadside bomb ends her first deployment—not to mention her career—she is left to pick up the pieces of what is left of her life. She's returned to Oceanside to regroup and move on. It doesn't mean she's ready for a relationship, even if a particular Santini has different plans.

Love happens when you least expect it.

When he first met Madison back at the Academy, Dante Santini is sure the woman was put on the earth to irritate him. She's prickly and mouthy. She always thinks she's right. Worse—she almost always is. She hasn't really changed over the years. One disagreement ends up with them lip locked and very nearly falling into bed, Dante discovers he might need to rethink his first impression.

When Madison is convinced she witnesses a murder, the only person who believes her is Dante. Together, they sift through the meager evidence, trying to unearth the secrets someone is trying to hide. Neither one of them expecting it would draw them closer—or that a killer is hell bent on making sure those secrets stay buried.

* * * *

Dante enjoyed having the fresh night air whip through Madison's jeep. Charlie was laying in the back seat, relatively quiet.

"I don't know if letting your sister run off with JT was a good idea," she said, pulling into his driveway.

"Aw, he's like a brother to her. He'll make sure she gets home okay. Besides, if anyone tried anything on her, even a little tipsy, she would be able to kick their ass."

"Hmm," was all she said.

"Thanks for the ride home, Mad Madison."

"I already said that." Then she chuckled. "I can't believe that girl calls me that still."

She was smiling and it was like that first day he met her. She was his sister's roommate and she'd been so cute…and sexy. So fucking sexy.

"What?" she asked.

"It's just…"

Before she could stop him, he leaned forward and brushed his mouth over hers. She stilled. He pulled back and licked his lips.

"What did you do that for?"

"I've been wondering what it would be like since the first time I saw you."

"You have not."

He closed his eyes and pictured her that day. "You had your hair up in a ponytail, all sassy and curly. You were wearing an old high school t-shirt, black and gold, and a pair of worn jeans that hugged your hips."

He opened his eyes. She looked stunned. "Oh, hell, I left Madison Baker speechless."

He leaned in again and deepened the kiss this time. Raising his hand, he cupped her face and slid his tongue against the seam of her lips. She hesitated then opened her mouth. He dove inside, enjoying the warm, wet comfort of her mouth. She moaned, the sound of it vibrating against his tongue and through his body. Hell, he felt it in his soul. He leaned closer still, pressing his body against hers. He was seriously thinking of inviting her into his house when she leaned against the horn. The blaring sound was like cold water. They both pulled back.

He opened his eyes slowly. She raised her hand to her lips and brushed them against it.

"I think we might need to explore this new development," he said.

She was shaking her head. "I don't think that's a good

idea, Dante. I have issues."

He snorted. "That sounds like an excuse."

"It is."

"Let's just say that you like to kiss me. I like to kiss you and maybe we need to explore this whole new thing between us."

"No."

He leaned in and stole another kiss. "Yeah, I think so, but I'll let you sleep on it."

He slipped out of the car before she could argue with him. He made it up his walk easily, but when he tried to unlock the door, he dropped the keys on the stoop. It wasn't because he was drunk. His hands were still shaking from that kiss.

ONE NIGHT WITH A SANTINI

He was searching for something that was missing from his life.

Brando Santini is headed to New Orleans to blow off some steam with a few of his buddies. The respite from his life as a Marine doesn't really seem to do the trick until he runs into his college crush, Kaitlin Fitzpatrick. After a little dancing and a few drinks, they end up in bed together and Brando knows she's the one for him.

One night will never be enough.

Kaitlin never forgot Brando. She never would have thought the sexy nerd would have remembered her. More than that, she definitely didn't expect he would be interested in seducing her. Their time in New Orleans is intense but much too short. The memories of his lovemaking leave her counting the days until she sees him again.

A complication neither of them expected.

By the time Brando arrives in Maryland, Kaitlin suspects that their one night together has left them with more than memories. When Brando insists on marriage, she refuses on the grounds he doesn't love her. But what Kaitlin doesn't understand is that when a Santini wants to prove his love, nothing will stand in his way—not her five brothers, his own annoying family, or even the woman he adores.

By the time Brando was seeing Kaitlin to her room, he was convinced he should get some kind of award. It was hard to believe it was taking more of his attention to control the arousal thrumming through his blood than it had in college. Of course, actually talking with none of that blood in his brain had been hard to handle, but he had pulled it off tonight.

"This one is me," she said.

He hated the tone she was using with him now. It was the same thing as if she had patted him on the head and said goodnight. He knew that she saw him as a friend. He had said something wrong during dinner, and she had switched off. Before then, she had been staring at him like she wanted him for dessert. He had been fully ready to play that role for her. Hell, he knew he wasn't going to get any sleep, but he wasn't about to go out. She was in his mind and tugging on his soul again. He didn't know if he would ever be able to get her out of his head now.

Brando knew he had this last chance. He was going to make sure she understood where they stood. She unlocked the door and turned to face him.

"I am so glad I ran into you tonight."

He smiled. "I think it was more that I ran into you."

She chuckled. "Yes, but then, you had issues with being too focused at times."

"Hmm."

Silence. She was trying to step back into her room, and he couldn't let that happen. She needed to understand that when he got to Maryland, he was planning on pursuing her, in every way possible.

Before she could take another step back, he rested his hand against the doorjamb and leaned closer.

"I can't let you go without a goodnight kiss."

She blinked. "Oh, Brando, you don't have to do that. I understand. It's sweet, but, let's just leave it at that."

That was not the response he expected. That was his only excuse for allowing her to step further into the room. She was already closing the door.

He knew he had to make sure she knew that he wasn't trying to be sweet. Brando stepped forward.

"I think you might be confused about something."

She frowned. "What are you talking about?"

"The kiss was more about what I *wanted*."

He slipped his arm around her waist and pulled her forward. He had the pleasure of watching her eyes widen in surprise before he slammed his mouth down on hers.

You met MJ's brothers in The Santinis, now, get to know them in their own spinoff novella series: Semper Fi Marines!

TEASE ME- BOOK 1

A man who thinks he has what he wants.

Bran Johnson always knew he wanted to be a Marine. What makes it even better is longtime gal pal TK is now stationed at the same base. Unfortunately, Bran is having a hard time dealing with his feelings when he realizes that TK is considered a hot commodity on base. Worse, he finds himself taking a backseat to her admirers.

A woman who always wished for more.

Tess Keller has loved Bran since they were in high school. The former football captain always treated her like a friend so she tried to move on. Unfortunately, he's in her business constantly now. One passionate argument leads to more than either of them expected. Tess knows it isn't going to last because Bran is never going to settle down. So, to save face, she suggests they stay friends, only with the side benefit of being sometime lovers.

A Marine determined to win at all costs.

Bran agrees to the friends with benefits idea just to keep himself close to Tess. She might think he's not around for the long haul, but this is one Johnson brother who knows exactly what he wants...and just how to get it. And what he wants is Tess in his bed and in his life forever. Nothing will stop him, not even Tess herself.

TEMPT ME- BOOK 2

The man who could be general.

Jesse Johnson is a man everyone assumes will be a general. Everyone, that is, but Jesse himself. He isn't sure if he wants to give that much to the military. His father has spent most of his life surviving a lonely existence with only his work for comfort. Jesse doesn't want that—he wants it all.

The woman who tempts him to misbehave.

The last year has been bad for Zoe Jones. Her boyfriend was killed by some nasty guys who then put her in the hospital. She's come to Virginia to heal not to fall for some by the book, drop dead gorgeous Marine with a chip on his shoulder. But one little encounter leads to a kiss and that kiss leads to all kinds of interesting entanglements. She knows it won't last because he has big plans, but she can't help but falling a little in love with him.

A Marine on a mission.

Jesse knows Zoe thinks they're just having a bit of fun, but he has other plans. Forever kind of plans. He's one man who knows how to organize a full on assault to get the woman he loves—and nothing will stop him.

TOUCH ME – BOOK 3

A man trying to forget.

Jackson Johnson had always planned to spend his life in the Marines serving his country—that is until he came back from a mission with memories he'd rather not have. He feels like he's circling the drain until he meets the new tenant next door. An altercation with her unruly dog has them at odds. That is until he finds himself kissing her.

A woman who doesn't have time for love.

Veterinarian Hannah Richmond doesn't have time for the surly Marine or any man for that matter. Still, resisting his kisses proves futile and soon she finds herself falling for Jack. For the first time in a really long time she discovers she might just want to try for that happily ever after—that is until her past comes back to haunt her.

A Marine determined to prove his love.

Jack knows Hannah is pushing him away because she wants to keep him safe but there is one thing she needs to understand: this Marine will never retreat until she surrenders.

ENJOY THIS EXCERPT FROM TEASE ME!

Later that night, Bran frowned when his phone played *Beethoven's Fifth*, alerting him that MJ was calling. He felt oddly deflated that Tess hadn't called, but he knew she was busy.

"Hello, MJ."

"Hello, yourself. How's the house hunt?" she asked in typical MJ fashion. His father liked to say that MJ was born talking, and that wasn't far from the truth. She was always half way through a conversation before Bran knew they were having one.

He didn't know how to answer the question. Now that MJ and Tess started talking back and forth on the phone, he wasn't sure how to proceed. Part of him knew he needed a place, and the house down the street would be perfect. But there was a bigger part of him that didn't want to leave Tess' house.

"Okay, still looking."

A beat of silence. And that was a bad thing with MJ. "You know you can't mooch off Tess forever. And besides, she has a personal life."

"I know that." Then he realized what she said. "Wait, has she talked to you about that?"

"What, that you're a mooch? Not in detail."

"Her personal life. Has she complained to you?"

"Nope."

Then nothing. She just let the silence stretch. She might have been the youngest Johnson, but MJ knew just how to control all of them. And one way was with silence. Even knowing that, he took the bait.

"What do you mean by personal life?"

"Listen, I talked to Jesse, who told me she is gorgeous. Of course, I always knew she would be. She was just one of those girls who needed to grow into her looks. Now, with you there, you could be cramping her style."

"Cramping her style?"

"Yeah. I mean, if I were her and working on a base with a ton of military men, I know I would probably be busy. Okay, if I hadn't sworn off military men like I had."

There was some kind of talking on the other side of the phone.

"Of course, not now, Leo. It's all about you, the sex god of my dreams."

Bran was amused and disgusted at the same time. MJ and Leo had a relationship most people would call just about perfect, but then those people didn't have to hear them be disgusting.

"Could you two not talk about sex while I am on the phone?"

"Better than us having it on the phone while you listen."

"Ugh, I don't know how you turned out the way you did."

"Anyway, back to your living arrangements."

"I've been here a few days. I looked at houses and apartments one day. We hit the beach another day. And, Tess has been working like crazy hours since then."

"Maybe you drove her away."

"I didn't drive her away. Oh my God, you are such a pain in the ass. Stomach flu hit the hospital staff, so she's helping out."

The door to the garage opened in the kitchen and he looked over. All of a sudden, he felt the air leave his lungs, and he felt a little off center. Tess was smiling and she looked like she hadn't had much sleep since he'd seen her that morning, but…damn, she was beautiful.

Every ounce of good sense drained from his head…along with the blood. His body reacted even if his mind hadn't caught up yet. Heat surged through is his veins and everything he had been fearing seemed to fade away. There was only one thing that mattered now and that was touching Tess.

"I gotta go now, MJ."

"Wait, I'm not done with you—"

But he hung up the phone. "Hey. You look beat."

She sighed. "I am. I think I'll strip down, crawl into bed, and go into a coma sleep."

His brain sputtered to a stop. Right there, right then, he wanted her. There was no denying it now. His body ached, his head spun. Never in his life had he wanted a particular woman this much. It left him slightly dizzy and confused. Over the last few days, he had denied his need for her so many times, but right then, at that moment, he couldn't. There was something about Tess that tugged at his heart. It was probably a mistake, but he didn't think he could stop himself from taking action. He walked over to her and slipped his arm around her waist. In that instant, it just felt right.

She frowned. "Bran?"

"I've been thinking about this all day."

He had been. Since he stopped by for breakfast that morning, he'd been thinking about it. He wanted a taste. Her mouth. Her flesh. Bran wanted to savor every bit of her body.

The moment his mouth touched hers, she shivered. He was enough of a man to admit that it turned him on to know she was vulnerable to him. She moaned against him as he pressed his body to hers.

Before he knew what was happening, she pulled back shaking her head at him. It took him a second to realize she was trying to disengage from him. There was a split second where he thought about denying her that. Not allowing her to go. Then, his common sense hit him. With much reluctance, he allowed her to step back.

"What's wrong?"

She looked at him strangely, and he didn't blame her. Even Bran heard the arousal in his voice. It vibrated just beneath the surface and pounded through his veins.

She took another step back. "This isn't smart."

"I never said it was." He stepped towards her, closing the distance.

Tess held out her hand as if to ward him off, but he took it in his and pulled it up to his mouth.

"Bran, you're not interested in me. You never have been."

"You're wrong there."

She rolled those expressive green eyes of hers, and he hid a smile as he nibbled on her fingers.

"I'm not wrong, Bran. I've never been your kind of woman."

He heard the doubt in her voice and was stunned. This woman had always seemed so confident, so sure of herself. But in this, she seemed…at a loss. She apparently didn't know how stunning her found her. That she was gorgeous inside and out.

He guessed it was time to reveal that little secret of his.

"Do you remember graduation?"

"Yes, it rained, we had it inside. It was hot as hell."

"Not high school. Annapolis."

She frowned in thought, then nodded.

"You were so excited that you came running up to me and hugged me. Do you remember that?"

She sighed. "Of course I do. It wasn't that long ago. I don't know what this has to do with the fact that you're gnawing on my fingers."

"Then you kissed me. On the mouth. You'd never done that before."

Anyone watching would have seen a calm woman, but Bran knew better. He was holding her hand and his fingers skimmed over her pulse. It sped up a beat or two. Bran was enough of a competitor to admit he enjoyed that.

She cleared her throat apparently trying to compose herself. "And?"

He nibbled a little longer, taking his time. He knew it was small of him, but he was enjoying her discomfort. "There's a reason I avoided you for a few months. For a second there, I almost lost it."

Now she looked very wary. "Bran if you want me to believe—"

Irritated with her, and the fact that he was dying to touch more than just her hand, he interrupted her.

"I am not lying. You kissed me. It lasted a second and the only thing I could think was that I wanted more."

Her eyes widened and she shook her head.

He nodded. "Thoughts of tearing off your clothes and kissing every inch of your body took over. Then, all the family came up and well, I felt perverted because the rest of the night I wondered what you looked like under your uniform."

"You ran off with Jimmy and the rest of those idiots that night."

"And I came back to the hotel without them. I couldn't get you out of my mind. Then, you were gone and we were both busy. It all hit me when I saw you the other day."

"Bran."

"It's true. I want you. And I could tell from that kiss, you want me. Why does it have to be any harder than that?"

"Our families, our…careers."

"And you date other Marines. Unless there is something wrong with me."

"There's nothing wrong with you."

The way she said it was as if she was irritated with him for it.

"Hey, I won't push you, but tell me…can you really say you don't want this?"

He pulled her closer and kissed her again, this time thrusting his tongue inside her mouth. She tasted of minty toothpaste and lust. It was an odd combination, but need poured through him. Then, slowly, she slipped her hands up his arms and behind his neck. It was Tess who pressed her body against his this time, and it was him who shook. She tilted her head to the side and slid her tongue against his.

When he pulled back, they were both breathing heavily.

"So, what do you say, Tess?"

He left it up to her. He knew that for her, it was the right way to go. Tess always had to think things over and if she said she wanted to wait, he would wait. He'd have to take a cold shower for an hour, but he would do it. She lifted her fingers to her lips and touched her mouth. She looked stunned.

Damn, she was going to say to wait. Or, worse, no. That would be ten times worse. But then, in a blink of an eye, she dropped her hand and her lips curved.

"Tess?"

"Yes."

"Are you sure?"

She nodded. "Have you ever known me to not say what I mean?"

Then, he let out an oorah as he bent to pick her up. He caught her unawares and she squealed.

"Bran, put me down," she said wiggling against him.

"I will, when I can put you under me."

Then he marched into her bedroom.

If you enjoy Melissa Schroeder's Santinis, try out her military romances set in the world of Harmless.

INFATUATION: A LITTLE MILITARY HARMLESS ROMANCE #1

To prove her love and save her man, she has to go above and beyond the call of duty.

SEAL Francis McKade never acted on his feelings for his best friend's sister. All that changes at a wedding in Hawaii, but the next morning, he's called for a mission-one that leaves his world in shambles.

Months later, Kade shows up in her bar a changed man. When he pushes her to her limits in the bedroom, Shannon refuses to back down. One way or another, he'll learn there is no walking away from love—not while she still has breath in her body.

Warning: This book contains two infatuated lovers, a hardheaded military man, a determined woman, some old friends, and a little taste of New Orleans. As always, ice water is suggested while reading. It might be the first military Harmless book, but the only thing that has changed is how hot our hero looks in his uniform—not to mention out of it.

ENJOY THIS EXCERPT FROM INFATUATION!

Kade's heart jumped into his throat when he saw Shannon walking determinedly in his direction. She wore her hair up to show off her slender neck and the diamond earrings he knew Mal had bought her. God, she was gorgeous. He liked strong women, and that was definitely Shannon. All the feminine strength in that sexy package, he was having a hard time resisting her. Everything in his body, especially one particular body part, told him to go after her. But his brain wouldn't let him. He couldn't act on his attraction. Mal was his best friend, and one of the things he'd always believed in was you didn't fuck around with your buddy's sister. Since Kade knew he wasn't cut out to be involved for the long haul, he had to ignore the lust that was circling his gut right now.

Damn, as she neared, he saw she was coming after him for something. What had he done? With Shannon, you never knew what would happen. The woman ran a tight ship at work, and no one, not even her trained-to-kill Navy Seal brother, got away with jack shit with her.

"Hey, Kade," she said just as the band started up with a slow country song. Even with the music playing, he could hear her accent. "Do you think you could dance a little two-step with me? I know you have to be one of the only guys here who knows how to do it right."

The way she said it made him think of sex. Who was he fooling? Everything she said made him think of sex. But now, she was smiling, those green eyes sparkling up at him, and he couldn't think again.

"What?"

She laughed. The sound of it sunk into his blood and

made his pulse do its own two-step. "Dance. You, me. Two-step. You haven't forgotten how to do it, have you?"

The memory of her teaching him to two-step filtered through his mind. It had felt like purgatory, stuck between heaven and hell. Her body had moved against his, her soft breasts pressed against his chest…he'd almost lost it. The only thing that had saved him was that Mal was on that very same dance floor and probably would have beaten the hell out of him if he had known what Kade was thinking.

"Uh...yeah, I remember."

She didn't wait for a yes or no. She just grabbed his hand and dragged him behind her to the dance floor. She stopped then waited for him to step closer. Kade hesitated, trying to get his brain back into the game. Of course, his little brain wanted to do most of the thinking. His cock twitched as he drew her into his arms. They started to dance, and he tried to keep her further away. She slipped closer.

Oh, shit. Just the little brush of her body against his had his cock hardening. He just hoped she didn't notice.

"I thought you and Mal would be off having a good old time."

He glanced down at her, wondering about the tone. There was a thread of irritation in it. She was smiling up at him as if there was nothing wrong, but he knew there was something she wasn't telling him.

"Apparently your brother had a woman picked out already."

She nodded. "He's a slut."

Kade couldn't help it. He threw back his head and laughed. Shannon had a way of talking about her brothers, especially Mal, that Kade knew was to remind them they were still just her brothers.

"What about you?" she asked.

"I'm not a slut."

She chuckled. "The jury's still out on that one."

"Your brother needs to learn how to be a little more

picky."

Her lips curved up at that comment, and he felt the moisture dry up in his mouth. God, he wanted to kiss that smile off her face—then move down her body, exploring every delicious inch of her. He knew her flesh would be sweet.

"I noticed you're pretty picky."

He nodded as he worked her around the dance floor. "I don't fall for every pretty face that comes along."

She said nothing. Instead she laid her head on his shoulder. The gesture was so natural it was as if she did it every day. He knew he should tell her not to. His brain said he should do it. But he couldn't. It was too close to what he wanted, what he yearned for. For five long years he had wanted her, wanted to feel this way with her, her head on his shoulder, her soft, warm body in his arms. He had wanted that for so long, he just couldn't bring himself to stop her.

It was bad enough he would probably have to take a five-hour cold shower when he got back to the room. Sweat slid down his back, and he had to fight the urge to lean down and brush his lips over her forehead.

He had talked himself into not doing more when she sighed and relaxed even more against him. Her breasts were pressed against his chest, and with every breath he drew in that sultry scent that was so unique to her. His head started to spin. His body started to duel with his mind. His brain was starting to lose when the music ended. The band swung into a fast-paced Hawaiian tune. His body protested when he had to pull back.

"Shannon?"

Even to his own ears, his voice sounded gruff. She raised her head and blinked as if coming out of some kind of daze. Her breathing hitched, and her breasts rose above the neckline of her dress. His gaze slipped down, he could see her hardened nipples through the delicate red fabric. He curled his fingers into his palms and counted backwards from ten. If he didn't get away from her soon, he would definitely lose control. There would be nothing to stop him from tearing off her clothes and bending her over a banquet table.

The wind shifted, pulling a few strands of her hair loose from the complicated style.

He cleared his throat. "Well, that was...nice."

Fuck. How lame could he get? She studied him for a second, her expression serious, thoughtful. Then in the next moment, her lips curved.

"You know where my room is, doncha?"

Lust soared. His body reacted at the direct question. Any doubts he had about her interest in him vaporized. She apparently thought there was no reason to hide her attraction to him anymore.

He nodded, unable to form a word.

"Well, then you know where to find me later."

Other Books by Melissa Schroeder

HARMLESS

A Little Harmless Sex

A Little Harmless Pleasure

A Little Harmless Obsession

A Little Harmless Lie

A Little Harmless Addiction

A Little Harmless Submission

A Little Harmless Fascination

A Little Harmless Fantasy

A Little Harmless Ride

A Little Harmless Secret

THE HARMLESS PRELUDES

Prelude to a Fantasy

Prelude to a Secret

THE HARMLESS SHORTS

Max and Anna

A LITTLE HARMLESS MILITARY ROMANCE

Infatuation

Possession

Seduction

THE SANTINIS

Leonardo

Marco

Gianni

Vicente

A Santini Christmas

A Santini in Love

Falling for a Santini

One Night with a Santini

FALLING FOR A SANTINI

SEMPER FI MARINES

Tease Me

Tempt Me

Touch Me

ONCE UPON AN ACCIDENT

An Accidental Countess

Lessons in Seduction

The Spy Who Loved Her

THE CURSED CLAN

Callum

Angus

Logan

BY BLOOD

Desire by Blood

Seduction by Blood

TEXAS TEMPTATIONS

Delilah's Downfall

HAWAIIAN HOLIDAYS

Mele Kalikimaka, Baby

Sex on the Beach

Getting Lei'd

BOUNTY HUNTER'S, INC

For Love or Honor

Sinner's Delight

THE SWEET SHOPPE

Cowboy Up

Tempting Prudence

CONNECTED BOOKS

The Hired Hand

Hands on Training

A Calculated Seduction

Going for Eight

SINGLE TITLES

Grace Under Pressure

Telepathic Cravings

Her Mother's Killer

The Last Detail

Operation Love

Chasing Luck

The Seduction of Widow McEwan

COMING SOON

Prelude to a Rumor Part One

Prelude to a Rumor Part Two

A Little Harmless Rumor

A Santini Takes the Fall

CPSIA information can be obtained at www.ICGtesting.com
Printed in the USA
LVOW08s2006250515

439714LV00004B/202/P

9 781508 817710